First Father

The Novella Series Red Paradise

Don Atchison

First Father

Editors: Natalie Owens and Elijiah Hardgrove

Book Cover Concept: Zach Feador

Book Cover Illustration: Elijiah Hardgrove

ISBN 978-0-578-03932-9

To the late Abel Edwards, my grandfather. To the late Master Victor A. Hughes, my mentor. They were everyday men that were there for me in my youth.

Special Thanks

To my grandmother, Georgia N. Edwards, I love you!

It has been longer than usual since I've written you and that's because I have been working on corrections my editor gave me. Now I'm finished and the book is about to have its final go over.

This is exciting, and I'm ready to see how things go once published.

Know that me being published is mostly because of you. And not just because you influenced me as a writer. When I was a child you also cultivated the entrepreneur in me. Allowing, and encouraging me to sell lemons helped turn me into a go-getter which is responsible for me finding a way to come out with a book on my own.

With me having a good wife, and being a little older, I'm grounded and able to excell. I'll be alright, grandmom.

Thank you for everything.

Next goes much appreciation to Robert Nooner, and Jason Weeks for reading over one of my final drafts and giving me the best advice ever.

Reb Scott (Doc), you deserve your own paragraph because your critique, and our arguments have helped not only my first book, but me as a person. You are my friend. May your books flourish.

Natalie Owens, my first editor, I know when you got my book it was a total mess. It was you who did the original heavy work and set me on the right course.

Elijiah Hardgrove, my final editor, you really refined First Father, and gave it life. You are the best I've worked with. I wish you the best in your writing career.

To Gloria Elnora Evans, the Writer, what's up! You came along at just the right time to touch and influence my writing style in ways no one will understand. I'm a little big man now ...

To my son, Everett, Kiddo, you are one tough trooper. You encourage me to be the best dad, and man. You have quite a sense of humor too. Thanks for putting your company, New Era Advertising, behind the marketing efforts of this book.

To my mother whom I am sure I get my tenacious, fearless spirit from, thank you. I love you!

Ah, yes, and to my wife, Shena (Butter), without you this book would not exist. You tirelessly typed, retyped, mailed, emailed, corrected, made contacts and so many phone calls. You did all the leg-work, and on top of that listened to my complaints and doubts. I love you unconditionally!

Prologue

I, too, will return to the dry dust no matter my trepidation of that impending, eternal oblivion. No sort of contrivances of an ever existing soul, will make it so. We are no greater than ants or fig leaves. Not religion, devotion to rituals, heart-felt sermons or passionate prayers heaped together from all the populated worlds will ever change that.

Men and women, as they are born, will come to the same demise. Which is death, with nothing afterwards. As the scriptures so plainly state, the dead know nothing. As the moments that slip by prove over and over, no one who has ever been hated or loved has ever come back, or will.

Until my time, I savor the blood of those that give me longevity and vitality. Occasionally I will dine on one of these special prey, along with the choicest wines as treat.

One must have periodic indulgences, and I have my preferences, my inclinations.

Age has given me power over men, and they call me god.

They call me god.

-Domm

I was a man of faith until a vampire revealed to me part of the living Vampire
Doctrine. Now I know that since the dawn of man's existence, our ancestors worshipped them as gods and goddesses. As a result, our holy books that speak of messengers, prophets and what they did, are loosely based off of these vampires. In our ignorance we know some of them as the Biblical Adam and Eve, Cain and Abel, or angels, or God himself. However, the true names of these vampires were lost in the anals of time.

Depressed after learning these things, I felt I no longer knew myself. The myopic world I was once convinced carried all truth, was no more. I was left to begin a new quest to intimately discover reality. I needed to believe in something again so that I could feel alive, and maybe redevelop faith.

Adam, the most ancient vampire is entombed, his whereabouts lost to all. Yet, he must be found for he alone holds a special key that can lock a door which demons of unimaginable evil and destructive power have come through to feed on vampires and men.

Adam's only living son, Cain, has a unique connection that will allow him to track his father. If only he can tap into the dark, sleeping secrets of his vampire nature, he can find him. If he can overcome the hatred he has for him, he will search for him. If only Cain can control the monsters that grow in his mind, threatening to overtake his will, then he will have the focus needed to stay the course. If only this old but inexperienced vampire can defend against the trickery of the demons, witches and their powers, then he will find the First Father.

Layers of awful lies govern the behavior of the human race. Our secret societies, unbeknownst to them, only serve the will of blood sucking vampires. I am only a man, and I search for something strong enough to fill the void in my soul while I live with these terrible secrets.

-Father Donovan Edmasses

Don Atchison

The Beloved

Ten thousand years ago, in a land called Kemet, long before it was ever named Egypt, or had Pharoahs, there was a very special King and Queen that ruled, and they were vampires.

The rotting corpses of men, women and children littered the streets of the ransacked city capitol. Kind, which is what the highest rank of vampires called themselves, also lay dead next to their human subjects. The Kind were distinguished from the Kindred, the lowest of their race, by their customary dreadlocks and nakedness. Kindred and witches lay dead in the streets as well; thousands and thousands of them.

The Kindred and the witch race had aligned themselves and attacked the great vampire Kind. The assault on the capitol represented the end of a long, bloody conflict wherein the Kind were losers.

Deep below the devastated city was the sacred Chambers of Domm, the First Father, Lord of the vampires, King of Kemet. Witches in tattered black robes flew down a wide stone passage with their long disheveled hair fluttering wildly. A number of Kindred traveled with them; some flying; others crawling along the walls or running at great speeds.

A few witches whispered incantations, others wailed like ghosts, or hissed with vehemence. They were gearing up for the final conflict, and ready to take the First Father.

As the witches and Kindred rounded a corner, the corridor widened by twenty feet, where six tenacious Kind awaited them. The vampires leapt, sinking their fangs into four witches and two Kindred.

The sharp shrill of the four dieing witches filled the hallways as the vampires drank. The dieing Kindred remained silent, yet blood tears ran from their eyes.

Hovering in the air, the Kind released their victims. They discarded the Kindred with special disgust, for the Kind were their makers and considered them traitors.

With unrehearsed quickness, and overwhelming numbers, the witches and Kindred engaged the enemy. One witch shrieked and spat an acid-like substance that dissolved part of the face of one Kind. Several Kindred were then able to take hold and drink from the old and powerful vampire, finishing him off. The Kindred had to be careful when they drank from their makers, the act could prove fatal.

In just moments the witches and Kindred tore the few Kind into pieces. Ripping the vampires apart was quite an effective way to kill them, at least for a little while. To ensure their demise, the Kindred drank from the Kind as well. The witches had been wise in joining with the Kindred, for at times the Kind could be impervious to their magic. And if injured, the Kind could recover at a supernatural rate. It took very powerful witches to destroy a Kind, and there were very few of them alive.

Moving at a more rapid pace down the corridor, the band marveled at the light cast by torches in silver scones as it reflected off the floor that merged into gold pavement. They knew they were getting closer to where Domm slept.

At the far end of the passage was a closed, great, bronze double door with emerald inlays. Twenty of the most perfectly chiseled male and female vampires stood defensively in front of it. They hissed at the approaching witches and Kindred, revealing white fangs. Flexing their fingers, sharp talons grew from their nails, while their eyes turned black and opaque.

One witch, taking the lead, gave a piercing scream. Some of the Kind grimaced and covered their ears which started to bleed. Only the toughest vampires refused to flinch, and instead, hardened their looks.

A female vampire leapt into the air and flew at the wailing witch. Her speed was so great neither the Kindred or witches could react, and with mortal accuracy she sank sharp canines into the witch's neck, cutting off her debilitating cry.

The two plummeted to the ground, rolling about in a tussle. The witch beating her fist into the side of the enemy's face with great intensity, the vampire refused to release her bite. The witch's life and power were quickly drained from her body and she died with an insane cackle.

Blood dripped from the vampire's fangs as she ripped flesh from the side of the dead witch's neck. Her eyes red as fire, she screamed in ecstasy from her fill, and craved more.

The two parties clashed. The battle was fierce.

Meanwhile, on the other side of the bronze doors: "I not gone leave me usband!" the Queen acclaimed. Her royal protectors lowered their heads in submission. "Take da crypt of me son instead."

The warriors all hesitated, giving one another nervous glances.

"Me usband is sleepin'. I am Queen, do as I say." She paused, looking over them. No one moved. "Now!" she demanded, and a number of vampires ran to and lifted one of two beautiful golden sarcophagus's. With haste, they carried it through a secret passage that was opened, then re-sealed.

Satisfied, the Queen sat on her solid gold, and jeweled throne. Her dark skin glistening, she threw her long and thick hanging locks over her shoulders and raised a defiant chin.

"Now let dhem come," the Queen sneered, and the two hundred Kind that were present, turned towards the doors.

With a shriek, a witch threw her hands in the direction of a vampire and a hot stream of fire slammed him against the bronze doors. He then fell to his knees with horrific, short-lived cries as the inferno reduced him to dust.

Like ticks, several Kind leapt into the air to take hold of a victim. Some succeeded, while a few witches were able to shriek and throw an accurate fire spell to incinerate an attacker.

Kindred were overwhelming the Kind. Witches alternated fire spells, some of which caused the opposition to internally combust. More witches and Kindred joined the battle. Their numbers were swelling fast, but the Kind demonstrated why they were to be feared, by drinking, rejuvenating, and defending with even more vigor.

The queen gave a quick grunt and a group of her protectors took positions before standing drums. In unison they raised their palms and waited. The Queen nodded, and rhythmic pounding began.

Leaning her head back, the Queen half shut her eyes and swayed to the intense beat. The drummers shook their heads and their locks flailed wildly. Chanting in the chambers followed. Only a few vampire sang at first, but the singing was contagious. The language was ancient, and only known by the Kind.

Dancing erupted. The Queen swayed. The drums beat louder. The Queen swayed, and clapped. Her voluptuous breasts bounced, and nipples swelled.

"Sisters!" one witch called in a high pitch. She stood before the bronze doors with her arms outstretched and glowing green.

Other witches joined her in the same fashion. "Sisters!" they shrieked in musical unison. With their glowing green arms outstretched, the aura pulsated, and the massive doors drew open.

From behind, one of the Kind sunk fangs into the neck of an unsuspecting witch in the middle of casting her magic. She cried as blood left her body, a tiny rivulet sliding down the side of her neck. Her body went limp in death.

Swift retaliation followed as witches swarmed the only remaining Kind and pulled his limbs apart. Kindred literally shoved and fought one another to be the one to drink from the vampire's throat, and when one did, it took in his fluids with unbridled hunger.

Well fed, the Kindred lifted it's head revealing red eyes and a bloodied grin of satisfaction.

More witches and Kindred filled the hall as the doors opened. Music coming from the royal chamber surprised the intruders.

As the doors fully parted, the music and dancing stopped. The abrupt silence was eerie. Not a single witch or Kindred dared enter.

The chamber was massive, with nine stone pillars covered by colorful hieroglyphics supporting the ceiling. Marble steps led to a raised platform in the rear where the Queen sat with a regal flare.

She was splendid to observe, and known to be far more dangerous than all Kind except for her husband, Domm.

A gold sarcophagus was to her left. To her right were the drummers. Before her, stood what was left of her royal vampire warriors. Their ranks were perfect. The ranks of the witches and Kindred were disorderly but swollen. Their number was no less than one thousand now.

Not a sound from either side was heard. Then one witch dared step into the sacred room. With a smug grin of victory, she wailed fiercely. Blood trickled from the ears of some of the Kind but none of them stirred.

Fixing a hand on each hip, the witch stated, "We will now have you hand over the First Father."

A pale skinned, slant eyed female Kind that was close to the Queen folded her arms over her breasts. Her dreadlocks swayed like cobras, as if on their own volition. "Ah, ya come for da faddah." She tilted her head.

Wailing. "We have," the witch hissed.

Looking toward the Queen, who only nodded with a smile, the pale vampire turned again to the witch. "Notin ere but dhat which would cause ya much trouble," she assured with a gleam in her eyes.

Again the witch shrieked, then each faction rushed the other with violent war cries. The Queen waved to her female right hand, who then nodded to several other vampires who headed for the sarcophagus. One quickly pushed aside the cover which was too heavy for a single human to remove. Another vampire slid a dagger from a sheath attached to the crypt. The blade was a foot long and jagged.

They were determined to let no one have the First Father.

Ecstasy

His name was Kheyang, and he dreamt of a time he and his woman were wrapped so tight, fused in every area that their bodies made contact. Her cries, his grunts. The way their limbs twisted, blending perfectly. The way his hips reversed then thrust inside her. The way her pelvis gyrated forward to receive the penetration. It was love, and they were young.

She whimpered with delight, panted and rocked her head back, digging her nails into his broad shoulders. Blood mixed, with hot salty sweat. It stung, though he hardly noticed; his tongue lapped at her firm breast, priming it, before his mouth closed around the nipple.

There were times they walked and said not a word. Yet in the silence love rambled sweet nothings. Her beauty permeated from within and to Kheyang, nothing else mattered. He could not be distracted, and at that point could see into his woman's soul where he discovered purity.

Their eyes often met and she proved to see deep into his being as well. No one could dare tell Kheyang that there was anything better than to have found such vulnerability, such transparency and sincerity. To him nothing was better than the love he possessed. He simply believed he had not known love until this woman, only to realize he had not fully loved until he experienced her as a loss.

Today, Kheyang hates, and that to him is sweet ecstasy.

A question posed: "Why art thou full of wrath and thy countenance fallen? If thou doest well, shalt thou not be accepted? And if thou doest not well, sin lieth at the door."

Sin's reply: "Murder can be ecstasy if there lives enough fire in the heart, enough anger in the soul, plenty of hate in the mind, and desire for revenge within every fiber of your existence. Give into me and be filled."

Jerusalem's Descent

Glory came from a northern cloud
Filled with fire and brightness
A beautiful angel, a man, a cherub
Ever-living and in the form of god – a serpent
Riding a splendid wheel
Drunk with sacred wine

I saw it
I fell upon my face afraid
And I heard an awful voice of one that spoke
You, you shall have eternal life, and be my nemesis

-Jormungand the Werewolf

Buried Treasure

It was cold, dismal. An hour earlier rain had fallen with violence, leaving the ground muddy and the surrounding green slopes, slippery. A handful of men frantically stabbed shovels into the earth, tossing mud and rocks into a huge heap while one specific onlooker observed with unbridled, burning excitement.

His eyes narrowed into slits that radiated pure evil while the lines in his face were as rigid as iron cords. He wore a black cape that fluttered recklessly as the biting cold wind whipped and wailed like a moaning banshee. His name was Charles Benedict.

The men hurdled more mud onto the mound as they continued their mission. The thick entangled limbs of the surrounding jungle concealed their secret duties. The region was a remote area of Vietnam, but that didn't keep the men on the watch from wielding their M16's.

This was their third sight tonight within a five mile radius. The others were failures. Over the years all the others were unsuccessful. False hopes of twisted men following an insane leader. One who had led them to this god-for-saken war torn country that had already cost several lives of their party.

But tonight; now something was quite different; electricity ignited the atmosphere. A calm resolve that this was the place pervaded the men. Some intangible force and the crazed look in their leader's eyes communicated that their luck was about to change for the better. And then...

A resounding thud as one of the shovel's struck something solid. The digging stopped and the men looked at one another with wide eyes full of anticipation. Smiles transformed some of the faces, followed by cheering. Charles folded his hands behind his back, pinched his lips together, and waited. The guards grew anxious and less vigilant as their attention went to the dig.

Lightning brightened the dark, clouded heavens with eerie silence, only to be followed by a distant explosive rumbling, like cannon fire. A moderate drizzle ensued and with renewed vigor the men continued to dig. Soon they were hauling a massive stone sarcophagus with the chiseled, gold plated image of a crowned ruler whose crossed hands gripped a great war hammer. Quickly the growing tenacity of the rain washed the dirt and sand off the coffin revealing its every detail. It was majestic, sacred, priceless. But the men seemed oblivious to the object's outer value and focused their interest on the crypt's contents.

Once the coffin was settled beside the grave, Charles gazed upon it with fascination. His blood pressure rose with his pounding heart, his mouth watered. This was it! And for a brief moment life seemed to stir in his otherwise morbid eyes. He closed his lids and inhaled the cold air, relishing the moment. Surely, a moment he would never forget.

Savoring his victory, he threw back his head so cold droplets pelted his pale visage, and outstretched his arms. His stringy hair clung to his face, and a noticeable scar trailed from the left ear and around the opposite side of his Adam's apple.

When his eyes flashed open again death gleamed from them. His men, who had been watching him with curiosity, seemed to jump back from that dreadful, invisible force.

"Bring the royal crypt to the plane," he sneered. Then he spun around, his cape snapped, and with long strides he headed into the darkness.

Scrambling to obey the command, six burly men lifted the heavy sarcophagus and carefully carried it away. They knew their leader had finally taken them to the one who would guide them to the First.....the First Father.

"I live because I cannot die. I cannot die because I killed my brother long ago when this world was very young. Almost new. Today I am wiser, stronger, and have murdered many. Enough to have lost count, and care not."

-Kheyang

The Chamber

The chamber was half lit by scented burning candles in silver sconces hanging throughout the room where a naked body lay face up on a raised stone platform.

"Oh incorruptible flesh, immortal being, eternal God, how long will you sleep?" The voice sounded like a dream to the one who lay motionless. Then his eyes flashed open and there seemed to be a moment of fear and disorientation dancing in them. He took in a deep breath as his chest rose then sank. It was the first breath he had taken in what seemed an eternity. He wondered, *How could this be? Where am I?*

A terrible aching in his skull threatened to return him to unconsciousness. His ears rang as a sharp, grating metallic sound caused them to bleed.

As if levitating, his upper body rose so that he was sitting straight up. He was surprised at how easily he was able to summon the power to do such a thing despite the stiffness in his body. Again, he wondered, *How?* The voice in the dark corner ceased to pray.

Surprisingly, his body had not atrophied over lack of use or nutrition after so long. His upper torso was still chiseled to perfection but his complexion was dull and yellowish-grey. His head was glabrous, so bald that his scalp looked as if no hair follicles had ever existed on it. Neither had he any facial hair. Not so much as a single eyebrow or lash could be viewed on his effeminate face. High cheekbones accentuated his quasi-exotic African features. His lips were full. His round eyes bristled with life even though they were grey like ash. Yet the intelligence that danced within them seemed to give light to everything he set his gaze to.

Wincing from another wave of pain in his head, he groaned as he heard, "Master." Charles slowly approached out of the shadows. Hands raised to his mouth, he looked on in awe and reverence. His accent was British, and his voice wavered. He wore hooded, pristine white robes and sandals. "Master, it is I who have found and freed you," he bowed.

Blinking frantically to clear and adjust his eyes to the dim light, he struggled to focus on   the image that approached, speaking with what were to him garbled words. Clutching his head, he moaned with the intense pain that cut through him, and Charles halted his advance.

It was the pain that gave him the strength to levitate from the platform and stand before the robed figure. Even slightly slumped, unable to stand straight because of what felt like someone hammering stakes into his head, he was six four and towered over the one calling him 'Master,' by at least four full inches.

His shoulders were broad, his neck long, and his frame thin. His pectoral looked like tiny vibrations in water. His feet, like his hands, were dry and cracked. His finger and toenails were yellow in hue and brittle. Well formed calves carried up to his muscular thighs and buttocks, leaving it as no surprise his phallus hung long and thick.

"And how should I reward you for this freedom?" He groaned and squinted as he gazed about the dreadful chamber, trying to adjust to the light. Contempt filled him. "Shall I bestow upon you, power?" His accent was pronounced and he sounded sarcastic.

At first Charles felt fear creep down his spine and the hairs on his neck and arms rise. There was something in the tone of this god that made him uneasy. Then a wave of reassurance swept over him as his lord unexpectedly placed a gentle hand on his shoulder and displayed a warm smile. The pain in his Master's sallow face was evident and compassion brought tears to his servant's eyes.

"However you see fit, Master Cain. I am yours eternally to command." Charles lowered his head in submission.

The words hardly escaped Charles' mouth before the hands of the one naked moved in a blur to twist his head. A loud nasty popping resounded, and the white man's lifeless carcass fell limp to the floor.

"As you have stated," he frowned, rotating his shoulders and neck to loosen the stiffness. This time there was not such a pronounced accent in his deep voice, but it carried a surreal reverberation of several softer male and female vocals.

For a brief moment he looked at the pale man who lay dead at his feet then he wondered what sort of time he had come to. The images from the man's mind before he murdered him were bizarre, hinting that the world had changed. He could only wonder how much.

With his eyes darting about he saw an exit and took his first brave step into a world he had not seen in …how long?

Cain? The man called me Cain, he mused. *Who is this Cain?*

Genesis

In the very distant past:

"Ya no I gone kill em befa ya made me."

"Maybe so," the other nodded, pondering with a frown. "But I in ya muddah believed ya betta."

Defiantly. "But now ya no I not. Whatcha gone do?" He raised his chin. Only his nervous rocking from front foot to rear, poised as if to attack his father, divulged his fear.

"Wat?" his father teased. "Ya gone kill me too?" He looked his son up and down as the young man tried to make him flinch with a sudden head jerk.

"If ya try in harm me, maybe," his son almost pouted. "Maybe I will take my ands in smash ya enuf ta stop ya." He paused, genuinely considering. "Maybe I won't stop, like wit Ablah." A threat.

His father grunted, "Na, dhere be not much good en ya, Kheyang." His eyes narrowed as he played with the long hair on his chin. "In ya tink ya powah all biggah din mine. Ya mukkle, ya. Ya gone see."

Subconsciously, Kheyang balled his fist as tight as he could, not due to growing courage but pure, unadulterated terror. Regret came next, but not for what he had done to his brother. He would do that a thousand times more if he could. He regretted the coming repercussions from his father.

"Blood cry up ta me, ya no dhis. So ya gone answer it good." His father popped him in the forehead with a palm.

The blow did not hurt but it infuriated Kheyang because it was used to belittle him, and he was a man now. He boiled with so much fury that with both palms he shoved his father in the chest.

The old man stumbled backward from the blow, surprised. It was the first time his son had ever dared to strike him.

Domm frowned, stood up straight and alternately flexed each chest muscle. Darkness covered Kheyang's countenance. "Ya put ya bruddah en dhere, so en dhere ya gone go." Domm pointed to the red earth.

Following his father's pointed finger with bulging eyes, Kheyang tried to swallow the dry spit in his mouth. His heart thumped as if it would pound its way through his chest. He felt flush, woozy. He believed his father was about to kill him on the spot, so he ran like a jackrabbit.

"Oh, boyaa. Ya kin run all day if ya like. Ya not gone fa. I in me angel, me brethren, gone git ya due, Kheyang."

Kheyang never looked back, but heard his father's strident laugh. It was the cackle of a madman, mockery by a god.

Where could he possibly hide in all the garden from the omnipresent eye of Domm?

"What ya gone do ta Kheyang?" Avv questioned casually while she lay across her husband's bare chest, playing with the curves of each muscle with a delicate finger.

The night was perfectly warm and the stars shone bright revealing their naked bodies as they lay in the tall grass. Earlier he had ravaged her body incessantly.

"I gone kill em dead," Domm said with no reserve.

"Why ya gone kill ya loins?" she prodded carefully.

Her husband quickly looked in her eyes, reading into her dark brown jewels. "Woman, wat ya say?"

"Em me son too. I elped make em en ya image. I ought have a say." She fell silent, and only the sound of the crickets played in the quiet. Then even that stopped, as if the insects could tell Domm was perturbed.

A cool gentle breeze covered them.

"Kheyang be cursed. But I aint gone kill em for ya sake, woman. No man gone kill Kheyang. But em gone pay."

Avv said nothing further, knowing she had stretched the limit of favors with her husband for now. But Kheyang would live, and with that a mother could endure the bad mood of her mate for a short season.

Yes, Kheyang would live.

Forever.

"The Lord is long-suffering, and of great mercy. Forgiving iniquity and transgression, and by no means clearing the guilty. Visiting the iniquity of the fathers upon the children unto the third and fourth generation."

-Exodus 34:6-7

Centuries

Still in the past:

When I woke I lay on my back in a confined dark space. The air was stale, stuffy, and there was utter silence.

Though I tried there was no room to shift about. I pushed upward, but the hard surface only pushed back. I ran my fingers around and felt nothing but cold stone.

Could I be entombed in a sarcophagus? Was I beneath the earth?

My breathing became shallow. I panicked, and a sharp pain stabbed the center of my chest. My mind swooned. The reality of being buried alive was too much to accept.

Did my father do the unthinkable to me? I would have preferred death.

At first I screamed but the cry left me choking, gasping for air that wasn't there. I gagged. The burning in my chest was unbearable. I whimpered as the fire in my lungs persisted.

Somehow I managed to shout, and shout, and shout until I was hoarse. I felt my body dehydrate like a sun baked prune. My skin became leathery, dry like strips of the carcass I use to enjoy as snacks.

My mind went blank. Absolutely cleared. Yet tears managed to trickle down the corners of my face. Partly salty rivers, my last human tears. I could feel my flesh as it chilled but at the same time I felt warm from the stuffy atmosphere around me.

I seemed to detach from my despicable self as I metamorphosed into a monster, and from then forward there would always be separation. Things would always be different. From that moment on, a division. A weighty reality would be my existence. In the darkness of hell I would dwell. While the brilliance of the world above would dance all over my grave.

That was the first day. In it was no good.

Mama, do ya no I ere? Does she? Mama, I Kheyang, ya son. Please show me ya beautiful face. Run ya fingers droo me hair. Speak to me muddah, I ya son. I ya son.

What I would give to rest wit muddah. Ta be wit muddah en be safe.

Do ya no I ere? Do ya no what dhem do ta me?

Not another moment. No more time. Mother. I often found myself thinking and talking in strange languages. My race were somehow able to absorb them from people we encountered. I had been told that on occasion we would speak in a tongue long before the people themselves developed it.

The second day was an eternity as I sank deeper into the abyss. I pitied myself.

Perhaps my heart did beat, but very slowly. Maybe I would die and be one with the earth. I hoped. I prayed for death. *Let me push forth as sweet fruit under the brilliant sun,* I pleaded.

Is there a god? Was there ever a god?

My people ceased believing in an omnipotent being eons ago. There simply came a point in our becoming civilized that we no longer required the threat of eternal damnation after death as incentive to do the right thing in life. *There is no god. No benevolent being. No meaning to anything. Nothing matters.* Not even that this was the third day of my always and forever.

No longer could I pity myself. However, I could close my eyes and dream, and when I did her face leapt at me in all clarity and vividness. Her flesh, unlike the dark rich earth, was like the white foam that rolled onto a beach from persistent waves. I loved her.

I loved her. I thought of her until centers in me I forgot existed made me feel something other than defeat.

Like she was right before me, I looked deep into her emerald eyes that sparkled like stars in the expanse. I wanted to lose myself in them forever.

Reaching out, I touched her body. The texture of her face, her neck, her breasts and nipples that I pricked had me yearning. The wonderful sensation of touching. She moaned.

Breathing, inhaling slowly. Oh the delight. Her aroma.

Then the curse. The dreaded reality. I awoke, or did I? It was still impossibly dark. An irresistible darkness.

No doubt I had been asleep, having a moment of the only peace I knew.

Running my finger along the grooves of my coffin. *My coffin...Possessive. My coffin. My, coffin. It's mine. It is mine. It belongs. Yes it belongs to me,* and I ran my fingers everywhere I could in my crypt.

The stone was rough but inviting. I loved it. I thought I loved it. I loved it.

I accepted my fate, my destiny, and snuggled into what would be. Until I simply fell asleep, enjoying the only freedom I knew.

My dreams, however, must have heard me and decided to take the only escape they had, for now as I slept I was moved, tormented even worse than when awake.

No, this is not true. When I awoke, the deeper darker reality was envious of my previous claim of freedom and proved sleep could be nothing but a nightmare. So the tiny bit of sanity that I claimed, that I possessed , that I cherished, that I needed, dried like a withered twig and I snapped for what adamantly promised would be the first time of many.

There is no god.

With a tight fist, I beat the top of my crypt, smashing my flesh until it was pulpy. I twisted with violence and cried out. I threw my head against the stone rest. The blow was strong enough to knock the will from me to continue. At first.

Insanity drove me to push the threshold of pain. I wanted excruciating pain in its purest, happiest form. So I ripped the clothing from my chest, digging my nails into my skin. At first the sensation was sweet, enjoyable like salting a lemon and sucking on it.

However, it was not enough.

Slamming the back of my head into the solid rest, again there was a strange thud, my skull had cracked. There was a blatant ringing in my ears. In my mind I was floating like a cloud way up in the blue heavens. I was an angel, and great wings sprouted from my shoulders.

Deeper I traveled into twisted bliss until unconsciousness claimed me to a world of oblivion, one without dreams, sound or random thoughts. I learned how not to exist.

Time now meant nothing, though this was the fourth miserable day.

Neither hunger nor thirst came to me. What was worse, I eventually healed from all self inflictions. It was how it was to be. But for how long? How long could I endure this?

In the absence of light time goes by neither slow or fast. Existing is non existence, and maybe a year past or single day. Half second, or a thousand years.

All the while I had only the words in my own mind to keep me company: *My name is Kheyang. I have a mother, her name is Avv. My father is Domm. My name is Kheyang. I have a mother, her name is Avv. My father is Domm. I hate Domm. I hate my mother. I hate Kheyang!*

For some reason hate made me slip and squawk a word from my sore, unused vocal cords. "I hate you all."

At first I was shocked to hear speech. Then it comforted me and my soul melted. I welcomed more of it. So another word came out. "Hello?"

I gasped, my chest spasmed. Tears, sticky thick blood tears welled up in my eyes. "Can you truly hear me, Kheyang?" *Yes*, was the weak reply I made in my mind. *I can hear you.*

Struggling to move a stiff, resisting arm, I ran a finger across the lips that released sound. They were parched, cracked. I spoke again, "Fingers," I elongated.

Yes, fingers, I thought! *That's it, they are fingers. Fingers are touching my dry, withered lips.*

For a very long time this conversation went between the voice in my head and the one that escaped between my moving lips until other voices in my mind began to chime.

I shouted. I sang. I shouted some more. I sang. There was an occasional scream but I doubt it was mine. I couldn't tell anymore what sound came from my head or pushed forth from my dry throat.

Voices danced, waltzed back and forth. Came, come, going, gone. Babbling abounded, mostly about nothing, and without cease.

Maybe this orchestra played for a million years. Sounds I had no control over burst from my mouth. Voices, chatter. So many voices and distinct personalities that I lost track of them all. All I knew was the incessant sound.

Insidious back and forth eruptions. Whining, gossiping, crap.

Stop. Stop it, I wanted to cry! *Shut up,* I attempted to cover the noise. But the cacophony in my head only mocked me by growing louder. Drowning my puny thoughts. Ignoring my wish, my desire for silence and peace.

Please be quiet, I pleaded soundlessly.

A response. *Oh, shut up!* it sneered.

Please, I can't take this anymore. Be silent, I begged soundlessly.

I told you to shut your mouth. Shut it. Shut it up.

Don't talk to him like that, another voice echoed, followed by waves of fresh debators going back and forth.

None of this is real, I told myself, shaking my head, knowing I had to make a firm decision. I needed to think. *Shut up. Shut up! Shut your mouths.*

SHUT THE FUCK UP!!!

There was silence, other than a last whisper of, *The audacity*, in my mind.

Not sure the hush was genuine, I remained still, listening, waiting for something to make a sound but nothing happened. I could hardly believe it, and I wept for the silence was so sweet.

Fear brought reason and I restrained my weeping. I dared not provoke the stillness with whining. I thought nothing, did nothing and lay there for a time in peace. All within the fifth day.

But of course after centuries of muteness, the tranquility itself began to beat like a drum. At first the sound was vague, something I couldn't be sure was there.

On occasion I'd cock my head, straining to hear it - this something. But no. It must have been my mind playing tricks.

An eternity of silence had taught me that it is true that the quiet has a distinct sound that only one who has experienced it can recognize. It is a permanent irritating grind sitting just out of ear's reach. Yet listen long enough, concentrate hard enough, and it is there. A lonely, sickening, hammering. Silent sound is incomprehensible to the sane.

And so I laughed. Not because I was tickled, not because I had stepped across another line of lunacy, but because I knew I had reached a special place of madness I had never visited before.

Picture the nagging constant weight of being imprisoned.

Lie back, close your eyes and exhale
Wait for a stone block to be lowered onto your bosom
Now push the immovable brick as you gasp for air
For relief that refuses to come
And the pressure with its supreme patience
Grinds your rib cage into grit
Think of a million people passing by
None bother to help
Some dare watch with amusement
The night falls
Not yielding any moonlight
Having no stars, just darkness
Not for an eight hour rotating cycle
But for eternity
With insult to injury mother time washes sands of each day over you
Burying your body
Not gently like rolling waves onto a solemn beach
But with a slap
Imagine slowly turning to goo
Black tar
Oil
The pressure, the time, the darkness
The solitude
The torment
The damned

Imagine, and you still will not have come close to the first moment I realized I was buried and alone.

So alone that I tore at my flesh with my nails. I dug into my chest until I felt nothing. I clawed at my face like a hawk sinking its talons into a helpless prey.

I stripped the flesh from my arms. I squished my genitalia. I pulled on, beat up my scrotum until the pain was in descript. I moaned with ecstasy, the tighter I squeezed and twisted, to turn my manhood into mush.

Throwing the back of my head against stone, I garnered a concussion. Chalky white foam filled my mouth as I drooled. Then I attempted to bite my tongue off. The blood was thick and coagulated with the foam.

My eyes rolled into the back of my head from the plethora of painful sensations. Then I lurched upward like a leaping dolphin, smacking my forehead into the stone top of the inside of the crypt.

Slamming my head from side to side only continued to crack my skull. There was pain, but after would come healing. The quick, unlicensed healing which angered me.

I scratched so deeply that flesh rolled under my nails like a lathe makes thinly curled wood shavings. Yet I healed again, faster.

I chomped down on my tongue. Pain…blood…healing.

"Noooo!" I shouted. Then I stared into the intense black space surrounding me.

For on the sixth day, I knew I was no ordinary man. I knew something. I knew nothing. I knew everything about myself, and I basked in this knowledge till there was simply nothing again.

Until on the Sabbath I felt a tingle run through me. It knocked me from my stupor, but not at once. I was so deeply engrossed and crazy.

Again, stimulus. What was that?

Upon concentration I realized it was rain. I could sense it as it fell above, and what a wonderful sensation! The whole ground was saturated, it was beautiful.

Oh how ecumenical.

Then strange images flashed through my mind. What were these things? The visions were translucent. Strange new languages were coming to me again.

As the rain fell harder all of my nerves tickled. It felt so good. I needed this. Desires of old rose in me. Forgotten pleasures. I touched myself intimately. I stroked my penis as it swelled. I pulled on it. I masturbated until that familiar scratch deep inside ignited, causing me to clench my buttocks. The feeling traveled from deep within my scrotum, up my shaft, and a thick substance saturated my hands.

I shuttered, welcoming the shocks that scurried down my spine. I caressed my manhood, milking every ounce. I tasted myself. I laid there in myself, sensing things above. Birds, creatures, creeping about. I could understand the thoughts of the beast of the field. They had fears, desires. Driving instincts. They communicated back and forth. They were intelligent, wise. Knowledgeable.

I could sense human beings too. They were hardly intelligent. Not so wise at all. Not so knowledgeable. What a wonder. Perhaps I could maneuver one to free me in…

Another thousand years, maybe?

Nothing but a moment in time.

Heart Throb

The Present:

After snapping his neck the pain in my head instantly quit. Up until then I could hear the blood gushing through his veins. The sound was extremely high pitched and ear-splitting.

With each beat of his heart my head throbbed and my only urge was to make it stop.

He spoke foreign words, but because of my natural abilities I could understand their meaning and knew clearly what the sound of my response should be.

Cain and master was what he'd called me. Curious accusations that, if not for the pressure threatening to explode my head, I would have pursued instead of killing with disregard.

However, he was an evil man. I could tell.

Voices in my head remarked in random, *We could tell. You did the right thing twisting his wretched neck. You did the right thing.*

"I did the right thing," I said.

Exiting the chamber, I traveled the dark stone hallways of an old catacomb. Some areas had only a single burning torch for lighting, but it didn't matter for I could see perfectly in absolute darkness. Some rooms that I explored were in disuse and disarray. I walked through stretched and winding corridors. Many chambers had only earth flooring and it felt good underfoot. After being buried for so long, my attraction to soil escaped rationale.

Padding in the direction of my instincts, I sensed the light of day above. Then suddenly I grabbed my head and stumbled before leaning against the cold stone wall. A high grinding shrill assaulted me and the throbbing in my brain almost crippled me. If not for being insane already, this new pain would have driven me there. All I yearned to do was kill to stop the suffering.

However, I managed to hide in the corner of a dark passage as robed persons carrying lanterns passed by without discovering my presence.

I slowly trekked up a flight of stairs in the dim lighting. At the top I blinked frantically, trying to adjust my vision to the brighter light.

Above were arched hallways and grand roomswith strange and unusual furnishings. There was talking too but I kept away from the people. Their closeness only increased the noise and pain in my head. I stumbled about clumsily.

Soon I came to the church atrium where many dust and cobwebbed covered wooden pews with irregular fading were arranged in rows. The exquisite, rectangular stained glass windows kept out the otherwise brilliant sun.

Spotting great oak double doors, I ran towards them and threw my body against them. Beyond this wooden portal was the light of day and fresh air. Fresh air and blowing wind I had not felt but dreamed of for many life times. I slid down the door, crouched, and wept with joy.

I pulled myself together and made up my mind that I would go through those doors. So I pushed my way into freedom. Powerful beams of sunlight forced me to shield my eyes. An uncomfortable tingling sensation struck my bare skin and I immediately stumbled back into the church.

"There he is!" someone shouted.

I turned to face the voice but all was blurry.

"All is ok, you can trust us. You're safe," another voice attempted to assure.

The sunlight had me partially blinded. My eyes were dry and burning. My brain, my lobes, felt as if they were separating from my body. Blood rushed to my ears. The pounding in my head made me lose balance. I staggered into the scorching light of the sun which seemed to fry my flesh. I howled like a wolf.

"Stay away from I! Me warn ya!" I growled in my tongue, falling helplessly onto my back. I writhed and screamed in agony. Without much success I attempted to shield my eyes from the sunlight with one hand while holding out the other to ward off the men that approached. Naturally they stopped, perhaps out of fear. The other reason could have been bewilderment.

Crawling to my knees somehow, I cursed the name of any god I could think of as the sun continued to scorch my body. Hate welled in my chest. Revenge. And there was the jabbing head pain that left me crazy for killing. My body shivered and jerked wildly. My blood burned in my veins.

I felt vulnerable and ashamed of it. I was totally helpless and that further infuriated me. However, my sense of smell was strong and the scent of my enemies intensified in my nostrils as their temperatures increased. The aroma was sweet and intoxicating.

They are all laughing at you, a voice in my mind swore. *You're naked, weak, blind, and they're all laughing at you. You are pathetic.*

I heard the men whispering. Maybe they were plotting. Maybe after all, they were indeed, laughing and snickering at me. Yet they were also frightened, I knew, because I heard their hearts' fast beating. The faster they beat, the more torture I endured.

All on purpose, a voice assured. *They are hurting you on purpose. They know what they're doing.*

Yes, on purpose, I agreed.

Then kill, kill them all!

Giving a mad man's war cry, I charged at my enemies with great speeds that amazed even me. Still I could not see, but my instincts guided me through and I grabbed the first, lifting him effortlessly over my head. I was power incarnate, totally in control. He deserved this for the torment, for my years of imprisonment. He was in on the plot. "You bastard!" So I lowered his back onto my knee and snapped his fragile spine.

The sound was magical. A sexual urge ran through my body. My penis stirred. The voice in my head had turned to many voices and they all incited me to, *Kill, kill,* they chanted with glee.

An attacker swung a wooden plank, breaking it across the back of my shoulders but I hardly felt the blow. I stood erect, flexed my muscles, and felt quite invincible. I turned to him, and before he could react both my hands were firmly cupping his throat.

Squeezing just enough to force him to his knees, I watched him gag. I stared into his face with my blurry vision. I could tell his eyes were bulging and I wished I could see into them with clarity.

His fingers tried to pry my fierce grip. Two men pulled on each of my arms while a third tugged at my waist from behind.

But my power was great and my will would not be overcome. They could not move arm or finger if I refused them. Desperation provoked kicking and blows to every part of my body. None of that distracted me from my purpose. My vision improved just in time for me to see the life fade from my victim's eyes.

Only when his body went limp did I let go, and then with a lion's roar of , "Yes!" I hissed like an animal, and raised a triumphant fist.

Ready to kill another, I was stopped short when a lit lantern smashed across my back. Hot oil and flames engulfed me. I squealed like a dying pig. The sound was gruesome, even to my ears.

Fire melted my flesh like hot candle wax. I fell, rolled about like a tumbleweed blown across open plains. The fire would not die. I supposed I would, and I looked up at the fuzzy figures that surrounded me.

I balled into a fetal position. My fist and feet were curled as tight as they could be. The fire had atrophied and constricted me all over. Maybe now I would finally die as I had hoped for so

long. No, I was already dead…but hopefully now I would cease
to exist.

> We'd kiss, and with eyes fixed on one another
> Our souls traveled
> Till our sweet lips separated
> And the world around returned
>
> Her hand fit into my own
> Our embraced bodies were –
> Like falling rain, cold blowing wind
> Twin to the aroma of the lathered earth
>
> This magic, even if a life traveled endlessly
> Would find only one soul in all eternity
> As perfect
>
> We had such a gift
> One that time and death separates us from now
>
> I can remember the exact moment
> Never more
> And the following second
> The next, as illusive time would, and could
>
> I am old now – Ancient
> But not her taste nor scent
> Or voice will I forget
>
> Oh the pain rumbles in my bosom
> But I will never stop loving her
>
> Within I have a special place
> Where I close my eyes and dream in darkness
> Where time is non-existent

First Father

Because time
Only cruel unforgiving time
Separates us now

Same Ole

When my eyes flicked open there was that familiar darkness, and I laughed. *Home again, confined to my room. My coffin. What had I done?*

My temples ached subtly. I heard voices in addition to the ones in my head. Three men whispered, but with concentration I could make out their debate.

"Why didn't we finish the job?" one sneered. "He killed Theodore, Christan and Charles."

"Are you kidding, after all we've been through? Everyone knew the risks. We must be patient. He is confused and this is significant. This is to be. He just does not understand," another insisted.

The third chimed in. "And I suppose you do," he jested. "Are you to be his tutor?"

"We must consult the Order," the one who argued for patience replied.

"Are you absolutely mad?" His associate fiercely grabbed him by the collar shaking him.

I pushed upward to blow the top off my coffin but the massive iron chains wrapped around it only rattled. The men at once grew silent and looked with trepidation.

"He's awake." The voice belonged to the one who had wanted to "finish the job". He looked with apprehension at the chains currently resisting the force he suspected the creature held.

Infuriated, I pushed harder. Nothing gave. Then I beat my fist against the inside cover and cried fiercely. The chains rattled and the crypt rocked. With haste the men stepped into the darkness, out of the torchlight that surrounded the stone coffin.

"Let us return to the church and confer with the others. We will take consensus."

The throbbing in my head faded as the humans went away. However muffled at times, my heightened sense allowed me to follow their conversation even after they left the cata-combs. *I'm sure practice would make me better in time,* I thought. *And there is always time.*

The Unspoken Order

The joints in Kheyang's jaws were stiff. They ached as he tried to open and close them. To make matters worse, a high-pitched whine was tearing through his ears. His head felt like it was in a nut-cracker.

"The men are all cowards," a woman purred, running a finger over the golden image of the sarcophagus as she sauntered about the crypt.

Kheyang shifted away according to her position. He grimaced with pain. He clenched his fist and grinded his jaw shut. "It hurts," he muttered inaudibly.

"Some of them are calling you a demon or devil. They don't really mean it. And I know you are not evil. No more than a sunset or clouded sky." She stopped circling and reviewed the mysterious inscriptions that covered the crypt. She marveled at what secrets they must contain.

Sitting in a wooden chair with an aire of grace she straightened the creases in her ankle length, brown dress. She wore black sandals, exposing manicured, red painted toes, and nibbled the tip of an index finger in contemplation.

"We don't claim to understand you, let alone your kind. But we know you are the master." She reached for the leather satchel that lay at her feet and withdrew from it a great leather bound book.

Opening to a marked page, she read in silence. Only the cracking of a burning torch or an occasional turned page sounded for the next half hour.

Her heart rate lowered and steadied. With it, Kheyang's suffering. He gradually loosened his fists and jaw. Controlling his breathing and with concentration, he further reduced the sharp shrill to a hum.

With the pain under control, Kheyang suspired. He wondered what the human wanted. He hadn't dared probe her mind.

It took all his strength to shield him from the debilitating effect of her presence. Instead he had considered what he already knew, such as that nine of them resided above, including the woman. She was the only female, and her name sounded like Selma, Serena, or Sena.

He also knew the party was clandestine, and practiced rituals regularly, some of which included the sacrifice of animals. There was also talk of a greater sacrifice on behalf of him. The specifics were vague. Yet it was disturbing because Kheyang knew a human was to be the victim.

While keeping his ears cocked over the past few weeks, Kheyang overheard heated debates regarding him. They were unsure about something, may have even been afraid of it. But of what he did not know. If only he could listen in with clarity.

"We are of an ancient Celtic Order," the woman interrupted his thoughts. Kheyang almost laughed at the statement. They were a cult. A silly, misguided order.

She continued: "From the beginning our people have known about and served yours."

An uncomfortable silence ensued. He offered no reply.

Tying her red flowing hair in a tight bun, she knew her work was cut out for her. However, she had made progress. No one else who had come to the chambers had been able to do so without Kheyang exploding into a tirade. For weeks she inched closer and closer until she was able to enter the chamber.

Arching and cracking her back, she moaned in relief. "You have many questions, I know. One who has slept as long as you must be quite confused," she trailed off. "No disrespect, my lord."

Her words were frivolous. But her voice soothed Kheyang like a cool hand on a feverish forehead. Companionship. He longed for it.

"My name is Serena. I am to help you understand what must take place shortly so that you can come into your revitalization." The last word she'd uttered stirred Kheyang's interest.

"You are Cain, our deliverer. Our protector. A guide to the Otherworld.

"The Celtic Order began straying from the old ways. Money and power became more important than the elements and belief in honor. They have totally forsaken even the most sacred way of the dead.

"So there are those of us, only a few, who have secretly formed the Unspoken Order." She leapt from the chair as she paced excitedly around the luxurious crypt. "One that practices the old ways, respects your position, and believes in the sacred prophecies of Claudius Ptolemaeus."

Kheyang was agitated at what he believed to be nonsense and sighed loud enough that Serena heard. He knew little of his people's past but he was aware that whatever planet his kind overtook, they were eventually looked upon as gods, angels or other mystical beings worthy of worship. This twisted stream of thought almost always inspired the indigenous people to form what they called, holy books, religions and rituals.

This "Order," he surmised, was such an entity. It left Kheyang disappointed in Serena.

Unsure of what the sigh was about, with greater emphasis as if to prove her loyalty, she passionately embraced the coffin. "We know you are the son of Adam. We know your father has gone by many names to many people. He is Odin, the all knowing. He is all powerful," she swallowed. "You have many names too," she whispered sweetly.

She kneeled before the coffin, mumbling prayers. Kheyang felt disgust, sensing the act, but pitied her ignorance.

The pain, however, was growing again as her excitement grew. Her energy flew inside of him. Liquid oozed from his ears.

"You are Cain, and under my faithful charge," she swore. "I will tell you things even the others don't know. This church holds many secrets." She glanced nervously at the entrance.

Suddenly, Serena returned the book to the satchel and threw the bag over her shoulder. Then with haste, she hurried out of the chamber. Kheyang entered her mind as she left. Her thoughts were scattered. She was afraid she had gone too far. Afraid that maybe the men had been spying on their conversation.

Kheyang sensed she had a strong inclination to free him and would do so with a little persuasion. So if being Cain would get him out of the crypt, he would be Cain.

Ragnarok

A tingling sensation alerted Cain to nightfall. He knew Serena would soon arrive and he was eager for her company. The physical suffering due to her presence was of no consequence.

"Master, promise to tell me all the secrets of the Other-world. I have always wondered what death brings. I can only imagine what mysterious beings dwell on the other side." She finally materialized.

Serena's posture was perfect as she sat in the chair. She was so well kept and poised that it was obvious she was a woman of upbringing. Cain smiled, he could see deep into the carefree side she hid well, and pushed further into her mind.

Having grown comfortable in the cold, dark chamber with Cain, Serena felt a sense of safety overcome her. She was convinced Cain would protect her in the event of any danger.

The more she spoke to him the more she yearned for a reply. She needed it as much as Cain needed her companionship. During the day Serena daydreamed about returning to the chamber. Could hardly keep Cain from her thoughts.

"Cain?" she stuttered. "Is there really life after this? The Christians, Jews, Muslims, every culture believes so," she mused.

Tonight her flaming red hair flowed freely like the pretty green dress she wore. Cain could see her clearly in his mind's eye. A trick he was growing stronger at.

He absorbed and savored her soft features. Her brown and wide bedroom eyes sparkled yet subtly hinted at buried sorrow. He could relate to hidden sorrow.

Cain's force grew stronger and mentally reached out to her. It was as if he stood outside his body. Serena gasped and jumped, and he knew she'd felt his hand lightly brush against her right cheek.

She leaned forward in the chair and peered at the golden crypt. "Cain?" She raised a brow.

Receiving no answer, she leaned back and inhaled deeply. She crossed her legs and rolled an ankle after letting out a stilted breath. She was convinced Cain had reached out to her.

It was alluring. Blood rushed through her veins. She was ready for whatever Cain had to offer.

"Let me tell you about this place we've brought you to. It is so far and different from where you were found." She scooted the chair closer in perfect sync with Cain's lipped whisper, "Come closer."

He could at times manipulate her actions. When their heart's beat as one as they did now, he experienced no pain or noise.

She felt a hand at her breast and sighed. "I feel your hand over my heart." Her eyes closed and head fell back. Strong hands massaged her stiff shoulders and neck.

"How?" she moaned, rolling her head. She shook as her imagination ran wild. "Remember when I spoke of the Vietnam War?" Clearing her throat, she composed herself. "In the jungles of Vietnam is where you were found. Searching for you, and getting you out of there was almost an impossible task. However, now you are across the waters of the Pacific. Here in the west. The United States, in the year 1969."

Neither date nor place meant a thing to Cain. When his people had first arrived on the planet the natives had scarcely developed their language, let alone an understanding of dates and geography. What was United States, or 1969? What was Pacific?

"This country is at war in Vietnam. It's terrible. All those young men over there dying, and for nothing. America is a meddler. We have no real business over there.

"You should see the protests. People are dissatisfied and willing to demonstrate."

Cain was able to draw from her mind some images of the incidents she spoke about but none of them made sense.

Serena sipped from a cold glass of water, ice cubes rattled. A wrinkle creased Cain's forehead.   He smiled and remarked, "Music."

His out-of- point remark pulled Serena out of her story telling. "Uh…," was all she could say, flustered. Reaching for the glass again, she shook it.

Cain laughed with joy. His wonderful laugh seemed surreal to her. Eager to please Cain, an idea had her hurry off. She returned moments later with a guitar.

"What would you like for me to play?" she had a wide grin.

Cain was inquisitive yet said nothing.

"Ok, I'll think of something myself. Let's see, I know some Elvis, The Who … Ah, and Otis Redding."

Serena started with Otis, then, pulled a couple of tunes by the other two artists and threw in a song or two she'd written herself. Cain rocked his head side to side loving every minute of the performance. Serena played so long that her fingers were stiff and her voice became hoarse.

"My, my," she chuckled as she sat back in the chair, lowering the instrument. "I've got to catch my breath." She fanned herself.

In the silence Serena basked in the feeling of satisfaction she believed the music brought Cain. She wished he were free. Wished the two could dance together, laugh together. Other thoughts and feelings crept in. Feelings she wasn't sure she should be having.

Fixated on the chains that bound the crypt, she ran her fingers over the cold links. It would be easy for her to -

She turned from the coffin and held herself. She huffed, and forced herself to think of other things. "We call the Otherworld, 'The Land of Faery'. Some of what we know is that your kind are guardians who sit at the boundaries between life and death."

"You speak of death as if it is a beautiful beginning. As if it is a place of consciousness," Cain stated.

Treading with ease, not wanting him to shut down, but curious to his meaning, Serena frowned. "It is a place of enlightenment and true freedom," she said with confidence. Then with uncertainty, she continued, "Your kind know this, and walk those who die across the threshold."

Cain held his tongue. His people's custom was that there was nothing after death. Nothing but what was experienced before life could be experienced afterwards.

"Your father is the senior guardian. He keeps the demons from entering the realm of the living. He will kill the one serpent who crept through and walks the earth destroying souls. "The serpent, that if left to his devices, will throw open the gates of the Otherworld allowing all sorts of monsters to defile men."

Paying closer attention at the mention of his father, Cain swallowed dry spittal. His throat constricted.

"Spiritual battles are all around us." Serena nervously glanced around the room. "Things that can not be seen with human eyes… We need your father. He will ensure the serpent is killed."

Cain answered bluntly. "My father no longer exists."

"No, my lord. He lives. Legend -" she started in a shocked tone.

"He is dead," he interjected. "Gone forever!" Cain slammed his fist. The chains rattled, straining against his anger.

Fear threw Serena to her feet. "But the prophecy!" she whimpered. "It foretold your whereabouts. Your father must be alive. He is our champion. The ashes of your kind were found in sacred places all over the earth. We have many of them in clay urns. They wait to be revived to help in fighting the serpent."

"Enough of this …this talk!" Cain spat. "Go away. Leave me. I tire of your ramblings."

A rush of adrenaline ran through Serena and Cain let out a monstrous howl of pain. The metallic grinding rang so loud in his ears that he didn't hear Serena's shriek. She bolted from the chamber afraid, confused and crying. Was all that she knew a lie? Was she a fool? Even worse, did Cain now think badly of her?

Oddly, Cain's thoughts were nowhere on Serena. Talk of his father returned old feelings of hate to burn in his chest. Hate for a man who had put him in a crypt to die. Somehow, the mercy of death had escaped him and he lived. He suffered for all that time.

No matter how Cain tried to recall the events that actually landed him in the crypt, he failed. Instead, thoughts of how he and his brother had explored the surface of the earth's moon as carefree, dreadlocked children came to mind.

Their father and other adults did secret work in mines on the far side. Work that neither boy was curious about because to them the moon provided all the excitement they required at the time.

But there was one day when Cain had stood with his father staring down at the blue earth from their ship. "Faddah," he'd asked. "Why da world dhere called Red Paradise? Don't ya see da blue?"

With a smile, his father had responded, "Ya will no dhat. But not dhis day, boyaa."

We do not age or decay. We are never sick, and are free from sin.

-Guardians

Little Lies, Little Secrets

"I don't trust the bitch," a man spat as he folded his arms.

"Kevin, you need to relax. What in the world do you think it is she could be doing?"

Kevin moved about the spacious kitchen. He was cooking. "Haven't you seen how spaced out she appears lately?"

His companion laughed to himself. "Serena has always been a bit weird. But seriously, come on. Loosen up, man," he slapped Kevin's shoulder.

Kevin did not give in. "Richard doesn't trust her either," he added. He pulled a huge turkey out of the oven. Then another. He turned around and removed his oven mitts. "Tom, open your damn eyes before it's too late. Serena is changing. She's becoming something else."

Tom laughed, but considered Kevin's comment. After some moments he shook his head resolutely. "Nah…changing? Now you're talking like you're crazy. You better not let Duvall hear you talking like this. He'll have your ass." Tom sighed, frustrated. "He'll have Richard's ass too. And you already know he's gearing for Richard's butt. And I swear," he said exasperatedly, "I don't know why you even talk to Richard. He's loony."

"Duvall won't do a damn thing. There was never many of us in the first place. Our numbers have only grown shorter. Duvall better -"

"I better what?" A hooked nose entered the room. The man it belonged to wore slacks and a cashmere sweater. "What are you two screwballs gossiping about now?" His eyes narrowed.

The two fell into a nervous silence. Then Duvall laughed, to lighten the mood. Kevin and Tom laughed with him, but with caution. Duvall was unpredictable and carried a violent streak.

"So…" Duvall glanced about then stuck a finger in a cake-mix bowl and licked it. "…I expect dinner will be served shortly," he said curtly. He raised his chin, peering down his snout at the cooks with pompous looks.

"Ten more minutes. Everyone can start to seat if they like," Tom replied.

Grinding his teeth and giving Kevin what looked like a warning glance, Duvall nodded. "Good," he said, and exited promptly.

Nine people sat around a long rectangular dinner table quietly consuming turkey, stuffing, salad, beer and wine.

"Pass the gravy, please," one man asked. His dinner companion reached for the bowl and handed it over. "Thank you."

"This is really good. I love the seasoning," Serena commended the cooks.

"Thank you," Tom smiled. Kevin grunted something inaudibly.

"Serena, why don't you tell us of your progress with the master?" Duvall smiled.

Chewing, she dipped bread in brown gravy and took a bite. "Well..." She dabbed the corners of her mouth with a napkin. "...he has spoken," she replied. She stared at Duvall, figuring he probably already knew about her work through his spies.

The others immediately stopped eating and the dining hall went still before an explosion of questions was thrown at her from all around. But Duvall remained impassive, with elbows leaning on the table and fingers interlocked.

Finally, his voice cut through the ruckus. "Quiet!" he demanded, and uncomfortable silence reigned. The men returned their attention to the plates before them. Until one of them crooked his neck and looked at Serena with a grimace.

He stopped eating.

"And you are just now finding it appropriate to inform us?" A wild expression marked his face.

Serena stammered. "It was only last night. It was such a surprise."

"Was it?" Duvall almost seemed to enjoy toying with her. "Well tell us, what did he say?"

Serena felt all eyes on her, boring through her. She considered some of the men were afraid or distrusting of her because of Cain. Some might be jealous.

She determined the truth would only be problematic. But to lie would be taking a chance if in fact Duvall had had someone spying on her meetings. She took a chance.

"He spoke of his father." Which was of course true. She just left out the negative specifics. "He spoke of the Otherworld." She reached for a glass of wine and swallowed a large sip.

"Will he lead us to Adam?" William, Duvall's right hand inquired.

Measuring her words carefully, Serena gathered herself. "He has spoken nothing of it."

"Why haven't you asked him about it?" Kevin spat.

"I never said I didn't. I said he hasn't," she scowled. "Time, gentlemen. This is going to take time." She was starting to feel more confident.

"Already it has been weeks," Kevin hissed.

A flurry of conversations followed.

"Quiet," Duvall spat, obviously perturbed. The talking ceased. "We have waited most of our lives for this. A little longer is really of no consequence." He stood. "And remember, Cain has slept so long. We must be sure. Don't forget I tried to warn Charles but was ignored."

The men mumbled and nodded.

"We have countless examples of rash behavior over the years. Do we not?" Duvall had every ones attention now.

He looked at Serena and she thought for a moment that he had grinned at her, as if he'd secretly caught her in a lie and wanted to put across to her that she owed him a favor.

"You take your time, Serena. Do this thing right." Duvall nodded to William, who stood, and the two men exited the hall.

A chuckle resounded. It came from a vicious looking man they called, "The Spider". Nobody could ever figure him out. He lacked couth but was dangerous and devout to the cause.

With butterflies in her stomach, Serena excused herself from the table and fled to her room.

"You notice the church seems to be coming -" William stopped and huffed.

"To be coming alive," Duvall finished. Their eyes met. Duvall looked amused.

"So it isn't just me." William looked relieved.

"A drink, old friend?" Duvall offered him a scotch. William accepted the glass and they both drank. "And no my friend. It isn't your mind. We are witnessing something special. And something quite unexpected."

Duvall walked to a window and stared out. It was dark outside and the woods beyond the courtyard seemed to emit a distinct threat. "This old church is much more than we thought. And I believe Charles knew this."

"I agree." William glanced about the den. "Do you really trust Serena?"

Duvall paused. "Nothing and no one can be trusted. There are those who would not have us find the First Father."

"Even among us?"

"I hope not. But caution is always best."

"What of the rest of the Unspoken Order?"

"For now they can know nothing. Not of this place. Not of Cain. It is too dangerous. And we haven't the means to defend against an attack."

"But there is the witch on our side."

"Shut up, man!" Duvall flashed. "Speak nothing of that old woman. Have you gone mad?"

William's expression turned apologetic. Duvall knew he was right. Even though they had the witch as an ally, she was unpredictable, had her own agenda, and was therefore - dangerous.

Only Duvall and William knew of her.

Seduction

Serena lay naked in her room gazing through the balcony glass doors at the stars and luminous half moon. Thoughts of Cain permeated her mind, visions of a future together as his queen. She believed him to be her husband and yearned for him to consecrate their marriage. She was determined that no other but Cain would benefit from her womanly treasures.

As she rolled onto her stomach under the silk sheets she imagined Cain's weight on top of her. She felt safe, protected, and fell asleep aching for her king.

In her dreams Cain slowly padded down the corridor to her room where she awaited him like an obedient, faithful wife.

The door opened as if of its own volition and he walked, gloriously naked, to the foot of the bed. He was revitalized and his rich brown skin shimmered in the darkness. His dreadlocks were pulled back into a tail. Her eyes traveled down his body to his erect penis. A clear, inviting liquid glazed the thick head. She looked into his face. "I knew you were beautiful," she whispered in admiration.

Whipping back the sheets, she revealed her fair complexion which seductively contrasted with the lavender bedding. She raised her knees and parted her thighs, rocking them open and closed, tempting him to take her. Cain's manhood reacted. His penis wept and she wanted to catch the moisture with her tongue. He smiled and she responded in kind.

She pried open her glistening core with her fingers. "It's yours," she purred. She threw her head back as she stroked herself.

Cain seemed to enjoy watching as she ran one finger after the other into herself, gyrating on her sticky fingers, pushing her hips forward and consuming each entirely.

Then she took advantage of her slippery middle finger and inserted it in her anus. She squirmed with gratification.

"Don't tease me any longer, take me," she begged, moaned, wiggled as she sucked on each finger, saving the middle one for last.

"Then come to me," he demanded in a sultry voice.

She lifted herself on all fours and crawled to the edge of the bed until her lips were less than an inch from the tip of his dick, which showed through the grip of his fist. Her warm breath touched it and Cain's jaw twitched. He drew a shaky breath.

"You want this?" he questioned her. Desire burned in his eyes.

The tip of her tongue answered by lapping his knob. He pulled away slightly and she grunted, "Come back."

"Come to me, and you will have it."

She did as he bade, her body drenched in sweat. Her insides pulsated. Her mind swooned. She was determined to have Cain, and threw on a transparent gown and went to the room where she knew the key was kept.

When she crept into the study and flicked on the light, the tall grandfather clock read five after midnight. Good, she figured everyone would probably be asleep. Only Duvall was supposed to know the hiding place of the key that could unlock the chains that kept Cain prisoner. Being Duvall's ex-lover, she was privy to that information as well.

Quickly she hurried to the desk and opened it. There was a revolver inside along with other miscellaneous items. Running her fingers beneath the drawer she felt for the taped key, located it, and pulled it free. She gripped it with both hands like she would a precious jewel, thinking of how soon she and Cain would be together. Even though she had no illusions about her being his only, she wanted to prove to him her loyalty and maybe she'd eventually be his queen because of it.

Turning off the light, she exited the room and closed the door. She was about to turn when a voice from directly behind her demanded, "What are you doing?"

She jumped. "Wha-humph?" She was careful to conceal the key behind her back as she turned to face him. "Damn it Duvall, you scared me. What is your problem?" She attempted to turn the focus from herself.

"Not so long ago you loved when I crept upon you." He pressed against her, parting her top with a finger, peering down at her ample breasts with lust. "Is it because I shared you with the others?"

"Duvall, stop it!" She turned her head away as he bent to steal a kiss. He had her pinned against the wall.

"From what I recall, you enjoyed that. Every bit of it," he grinned. She frowned, refusing to look at him. He stepped away. "Why have things between us been so cold these last few months? Tell me what it is that I've done."

She threw a harsh glare at him then softened before saying, "It's not you." Then she slid away. Cain was calling. His voice was clear in her mind. "I'm just going through some things. Let me-" She whispered, exasperated. "Let me go, please." She made to leave, was careful to hold her arms across her chest while concealing the key.

Duvall stared at the outline of her hips, thinking about the times he gave them a good ride. Thinking of the time they all gave her a good ride including Charles and their other two dead friends. Dead because of Cain, he frowned.

As a matter of fact, ever since Cain came into the picture, everybody had been different. Especially Serena, who eventually convinced them to allow her to teach him. She wanted to slowly help him to adjust because who knew how long he had been buried. According to Serena she had broken ground with Cain. She claimed he spoke with her. Although when Duvall or any other approached the chamber Cain erupted into a tirade, bouncing and rocking the heavy coffin, straining the iron chains.

Hopefully Serena would turn him around and they could perform the revitalization ritual to invigorate him so that he could lead them to Adam.

Wait a minute - Thoughts flashed through Duvall's mind. *The key!* Darting into the office he snatched open the drawer and reached underneath, only to find it missing.

"No, no, no," he cursed. "Serena, no!" he shouted, pulling the hand gun out of the drawer. "Serena!" he bellowed, racing down the hall.

William stumbled out of his room while slipping on a pair of pants. "What the hell is going on?"

"She's going to release Cain," Duvall shouted.

"Who, who is?" another questioned, scrambling to load a twelve gauge shotgun.

"Serena." Duvall was frantic.

"I knew it!" Kevin loaded an M-16 cartridge.

All eight men hurried, armed to their teeth. Duvall held a torch as they made their way to the chamber where Cain was kept. Their minds raced, mostly with fear.

When the men arrived Serena had just unlocked the last loop from around the crypt.

"Serena!" Duvall cried. "Get away from there." All the men with him pointed their weapons except Duvall.

Serena ignored his warnings, and slowly the heavy stone top slid to the side. Cain stood, ghostly grey and ghoulish in appearance. One eye was melted shut from the fire. The rest of his flesh was charred, emaciated.

"Duvall?" Kevin questioned. "We don't know what he will do."

Duvall stepped forward with the torch held high and his weapon down. "Master Cain," he called softly.

Cain's head was pounding with ferocity. Globs of blood oozed from his ears. His movements as he climbed from his sepulcher were choppy. Nine heart beats were driving him to kill. The sharp high pitch grind was too much. He could not understand the man who held the torch. The words were all mixed up, garbled. Strange.

Infatuated, the woman moved forward, arms out, wanting to embrace. Cain's mind was swirling, but still he knew he did not want to harm the woman.

"Duvall, I don't think he's listening to you." One of the men clicked his M-16 to burst.

Another of the men, who held a shot gun, stumbled as they were spreading out and his finger squeezed the hair trigger. Pellets tore through Serena and Cain. The latter's body hardly even jerked, but Serena stumbled helplessly into Cain's arms and breathed her last breath as she whimpered his name.

Cain's grey eye went pitch black as he looked at the others. He waved a hand and the torch was blown out, along with the others in the room. Gun blasts exploded. Men shouted with fury as they engaged their triggers. An orchestra of weapon fire ensued, along with shouts and screams of death as Cain broke and beat, pummeled, and literally ripped the men into pieces.

Whole chunks of flesh were torn out of Cain by the rounds. But very slowly, over the weeks he somewhat healed. He ached inside over the loss of the woman, which made him think of another time, another woman. One he loved like no other.

Immortal Love

Her love makes me immortal
Therefore her sweet flesh that I love to lick
Firm nipples I taste
Lips I ravish
Her round hips I roll about
I look past it all
To that part of her
That invisible, permanent area
Which is all I see
All I want
All I need

First Father

Having lost the luxury to die
Am I incapable of human emotion?
No, I am not
What I feel has intensified
Has taken me through the centuries

I am bewitched
Under a power
Binding, relentless force

I am in perfect love
And because I am a vampire
I am in love forever

Reflections

Even when buried with literally the weight of the earth covering my body, with thousands of years of torment behind and eternity in front, something inside my soul kept me believing I would someday be free. But that didn't lessen the agony of the journey. My experience was beyond description. And when raised from my tomb I hadn't even the solace of knowing I could exact revenge because those who did this to me, those I hated so thoroughly, were no doubt long gone.

-Kheyang

Still drained after the conflict, I lay among the dead. The stench of rotting corpses and their excrement was wonderful. *Something is wrong with me.*

Selfish bastard. Always making it about you, ran through my mind in a woman's voice. "What of the rest of us?" the voice flowed through my lips.

I shook my head, exasperated at the fact that I was not only talking to myself again, but now in a woman's tone. *Something is wrong with me.*

I continued to enjoy the company of the dead, wondering why Serena had to die. Then in my mind sounded the menacing hiss of a male. *We lay here wallowing in sorrow over a decaying bitch who served her purpose. We are free now. She sacrificed herself for us as she should have.*

Now get your ass up and leave this hell hole, another voice in my head added.

Something is wrong with me.

Shhh. Shhh. Shhh. Shhh. Cain's leg dragged as he arduously made his way out of the catacombs. Bullets that had riddled his body earlier had nearly torn away his leg at the hip.

Pockets of flesh where other rounds entered and exited, were sunk or hanging in clumps of infection and odor. That incredible power which kept him alive, healed him slow. He could not return to being the man he was before. He was left partially crippled, severely scarred and moved about stiffly, awkwardly, like the undead.

Lying low on his belly he clawed his way up the flight of stone steps that separated the world of the catacombs from the inner church. The bright light penetrating down as he struggled to ascend, it seemed to call, "Cain."

"Cain." An image stood in the doorway, obscured by the rays of light streaming past. With arms raising, beckoning, it said, "Cain, come."

"Who is it?" he cried out. "Who are you?" He blinked and squinted at the blinding rays. Straining to hold his head up, he blinked again but the person was gone. Yet Cain's vampire senses detected a force just beyond the landing above. Out of view.

The brilliant light was dim once he reached the top of the stairs. Only a single wall light lit the arched hallway that led into darkness.

Exhausted, Cain rolled onto his back then cackled in a crazed fit. But the image of something reflecting in a standing bronze-framed mirror silenced him. It was no laughing matter.

Scrambling to pull himself up using a nearby table, he shifted his weight to his better leg. Pain associated with standing faded. Cain trembled in fear as he stared at the monster reflected before him in the mirror.

Something was terribly wrong with him after all. One eye was fused shut with a green, sticky substance oozing from the corners. His skin was a variation of ash color and ugly black and purple splotches. Some of it melted in folds of rubbery, useless, and cantankerous infection. Patches of hair were napped on his scalp, adding to his freakishness.

A voice in Cain's mind screamed, aghast, and Cain found himself howling in unison, stumbling back. As if he could escape what he was. Losing his footing, he fell to the floor, drawing his knees to his chest as he rocked.

He wept. He giggled girlishly. He cursed himself, his father.

I am grotesque, he thought.

You are a fucking zombie. A ghoul.

I want to die, he pleaded within.

Fool, we are already dead. We are now in hell.

Leave him be. Can't you see he is suffering?

Curse him! Curse him good.

He flashed a look down the corridor. Something had been staring at him, he was sure of it. *A being. A human?* Cain peered down the hall, deep into the darkness. He saw nothing. Yet could feel the energy of something. Something tricky. Something watchful. He was not alone in the house. It was not afraid of him.

Cain sniffed the air, catching nothing but the putrid scent from below. "I will find you," he mumbled. *Him, her, it?* He contemplated.

Hobbling down the hall to a dark intersection, he traveled east, supposing it would take him to the rear of the church.

He passed great rectangular, half-drawn windows that revealed a dark, clouded sky. Cain sensed it was about noon, and wondered if it would be safe to go out since there were clouds blocking the direct sunlight.

Coming to an outside patio with an awning, he reviewed the landscape. Before him was a cemetery, lined with oversized granite headstones. Time had reduced a few stones to toppled pieces of useless rock. Weeds and brush graced the unkempt graveyard. Several wolves foraged about obviously unaccustomed to disturbances, for when they saw Cain he sensed aggravation by his presence.

One or two of the wild dogs eyed him. One caught a squirrel and swallowed it with a chomp. Another peed on a gravesite. Then before long they ran off into the patches of drifting fog.

A rock's toss beyond the cemetery was a mausoleum, overtaken by tangled brush, weeds, and vines that looked like varicose veins. Beyond that were foggy woods that circled the estate.

Cain stared over the graves as he approached the graveyard. Evidently the clouds did protect him. But he felt a tingling sensation run down his spine, and it did not come from the sun. It was the feeling of dread.

Cain stood in the middle of the graveyard surrounded by about fifty burial spots. He could not stand the reminder of being buried. Frantic, his stare went from headstone to headstone as that tingling sensation in his spine turned to a burning sensation in his chest.

He glanced to the right, sensing a wolf. Then to the left. They were maneuvering in the fog, attempting to circle him. And there were many more than before.

Afraid of a fight in his weakened state, Cain slithered along dragging his leg...*shhh -shhh-shhh*...back to the catacombs, back to his ossuary where he crept inside and pulled over that gold covering.

He slept, and slept. While the nine bodies around him stank. While the wolves above hunted. While that observer in the church waited.

Something is wrong with me.

She was my wife
My life and everything
 Yet our world's were far apart
And our destinies not permanently intertwined
I loved her
Love her

Don Atchison

Miss her
Search for her at all times
In all things
Aching is the only permanence I know

Breathtaking

For seven days, nine hours, fifteen minutes, and twenty seconds, I slept. Somehow I was developing an omniscience for time.

Climbing out of my coffin, I was eager to explore the church, curious of the secrets hidden within that Serena had spoken. I also hoped to find tools. My intentions were to dig up the bodies in the cemetery and bring them to rest with me. The nine corpses and I, hadn't much in common and I grew bored of their company. But those buried in the graveyard, we were kin.

My left leg was still cumbersome, but better, and so the journey into the church was not so difficult. However, on the landing I refused to look at the mirror. Instead, I shattered it with a fist in passing.

The sun was brilliant with the drapes open, so carefully I drew them shut along the way. Just as the hall went dark, I felt what seemed like a warm hand touch my shoulder.

Quickly I reached for the hand and whirled about. But there was no one, nothing there. I peered into the darkness. Maybe there was something. Perhaps it was a ways off, staring at me. I thought I could make the silhouette of a woman standing. Or was my only good eye playing tricks? Were the voices in my head becoming corporal?

When I flicked the light switch on in the first room, ugly rats scattered for cover among old stacked furniture in one corner. Dust graced the wooden floor, and thick cobwebs abounded. I tore through the silk, sticky threads as I crossed the creaky floor, and I made my way to a line of paintings that ran against the far wall.

I lifted one. It depicted a young, slant-eyed man with a ribbon-tied ponytail. He wore an odd, long, wide-sleeved robe-like outfit. Two swords rested on his left hip, one longer than the other. His chin was high. His stare, intense and full of courage;

though he did not seem arrogant. He carried the type of confidence that could have only come from experience, which seemed impossible for his youthful appearance.

"All is not what it seems." The voice came from the canvass. I dropped the artwork, surprised when I gazed at the youth and he nodded. Then when the painting went still the character was fixed with a slight grin. I rubbed my temples, closing my eye. My head throbbed, and I was sure I was seeing things.

I pulled another painting. From it, the menacing gaze of a woman who sat on a throne followed me.

"Who are you?" I questioned.

Her chin rose and she peered down her nose at me. I was quite astonished, and returned the dusty frame just as the lighting flickered. Then the ceiling creaked and the inner walls knocked. Was it the one who had been spying on me at every opportunity, and always at a cowardly distance? Was my stalker human? Did it mean me no harm? At least for now, I felt safe.

Another room was filled not only with cobwebs, dust and rats, but wrapped and boxed artifacts, some of which were delicate, and I supposed of considerable age and value.

Pulling from one container a silver tea kettle, I smiled at it's beauty until I noticed my horrible reflection. But I didn't look away. The oblong image mesmerized me. I was healing. My bad eye, I could now partially open, yet I could yet see nothing out of it.

Still I was a monster. But why, how had I become this?

From another box I withdrew a platinum staff with the head of a serpent. Tiny glittering rubies were inlaid as the eyes of the beast. The slick, protruding, split tongue was gold, as were the menacing fangs. The shaft was oak and scaly. The entire item was exquisite.

"Cain," a voice called. I turned, dropping the staff. There was no one. But where the staff lay a sound came. Then it moved! A ten-foot cobra, swaying back and forth.

"What sort of magic?" I muttered. The power of mother was strong in this house, I decided, careful of the snake's multiple strikes.

When I grabbed the aggressive reptile, it immediately became a staff again. I wrapped it in the fine linen I found it in, and replaced the weapon.

A fancy dagger with a sharp, curved blade and jeweled hilt seemed to call me too. I was drawn to it. It sat on a crate in a glass case. I opened it and withdrew the knife. Images flashed before me. My legs wobbled. My mind swooned. I choked, fell to one knee.

What ran before my vision was the distant past. Everyone ever killed with the instrument flashed before me like a play. All were sacrificed in bizarre rituals to gods that existed only in the minds of madmen.

I threw the weapon to the floor, disgusted.

Perusing the room, I opened an unassuming chest filled with gold coins. I closed it back, un-interested.

I found tools, shovels, picks, everything needed for digging. Taking a shovel and pick, I hurried to the patio and sat under the covering. The sun was setting on the opposite side of the church behind me.

With the sun totally down and a slight but icy breeze, blankets of fog rolled in. I loved the cold. Above, only a half moon shone between drifting white clouds. It seemed to wink at me, giving me approval to go to work.

Dragging my one bad leg, with a tool over each shoulder, I stopped in the center of the graveyard. Dropping the tools, I spread my arms and took in a deep breath.

I smelled life. Strange, for the buried were just as dead as the rotting bodies that lay sprawled around my sarcophagus in the catacombs.

I stared at the tombstone before me. It read: He sent men on before him so as to have company in hell.

Chuckling, I couldn't help but read another: Like a Phoenix, she rose to heights. She purified herself through fire. She sleeps, and awaits resurrection.

A thick patch of fog rolled over me. The mist was electrifying. I inhaled. My body tingled as droplets of water formed on my nakedness. I felt stronger, and stabbed the shovel with urgency. I was anxious to view my new friend.

A silvery moon ray illuminated me. This was meant to be.

"Ahhhh--oooooohhhh!!" a wolf howled in the distance. The sound was musical but full of threats. I breathed in deeply and was assaulted by a plethora of unidentifiable smells. Other wolves howled as if led by a conductor. It was a hungry howl, rallying cry.

Standing at about two feet in depth, with a worm-filled heap of soil growing along side of me, I knew I now had purpose in life.

I also knew I was insane, and perfectly demented.

Looking up, I realized all sounds had ceased. Something with stealth used the fog and tombstones as cover. I gripped the shovel as a weapon, holding it ready to swing.

Birds flapped their wings and prattled, whizzed by overhead. But something crawled towards me. It crept, and I made out an oddly shaped silhouette as the fog cleared twenty feet away. It was -

From behind me I heard a growl. I turned in time to avoid the snapping canines of a huge wolf. Swinging the shovel out of reflex, I split its snout in two, splattering bright red blood over several headstones.

Another dog helped itself to my bad leg as I was too slow at withdrawing it from its attack. I screamed from the pain, almost losing balance. Other wolves rushed in from all angles, five in total. I was to be dinner but I wasn't going down easily.

Or so I thought. One vicious dog leapt towards my chest and the force put me flat on my back. The beast mounted me, overtook me. All I heard was growling, all I felt was pain. I squeezed its throat as it snapped at my face.

I twisted the animal's neck like a cork-screw until the bones popped. But the other wolves tore at me. I actually heard the ripping sounds of my flesh. Yet strangely, I no longer felt a thing. What I figured, after all I'd been through, was that I'd now die by the jaws of wolves.

Thrusting with all my might, my hand plunged through the chest plate of one beast and I yanked out its beating heart. For an instant it pulsated between my clenched fist before sputtering out. Were there four or five left? No, six, two others joined the party and were supping, drooling, growling, eating into me.

Making it to one knee, I cupped my fingers together into a single fist and smashed downward, crushing the head of one. I heard its skull crack and saw its eyeballs pop out.

Five.

Taking another by the snapping jaws, I separated them. Flesh tore and bones popped. The mutt squealed.

Four.

Standing, I took the time to notice the bare bone showing in my bad leg as one animal wildly stripped flesh away with its teeth and claws. Or was that my good leg?

Damn, both legs were missing chunks of flesh. Wolves attached to me like leeches, flesh eating parasites, swallowing me in whole parts.

With an angry roar and single blow I knocked one hound thirty feet into the air. It came down on its side, square on a headstone, snapping its spine.

Three.

I groveled for the shovel and bashed another in the head over and over, gore splattering everywhere. It was dead, and still I struck, out of my mind, fixated. Then I realized the grip I had on the shovel was awkward. Everything moved in slow motion. It was as if I stood outside my body staring at it all. Wolves lay dead around me, patches of fog drifted, the half moon was still.

With that weird sensation still present I looked at my gory hands and discovered two of the last digits on my right hand missing.

Two wolves left, and I was a furious man! I snatched one wolf by the tail and flung it so great a distance it simply disappeared.

One.

Off into the fog ran the final aggressor, defeated. I would have loved to rip the stomach out of the beast.

I fell first to my knees, then rolled on my side and back, physically sapped and twitching in waves of pain. I closed my eye. Crickets sang. A cool breeze rushed across me. I could not crawl to the church, and knew what that meant.

The first thread of colored light was breathtaking and surreal. I hadn't viewed a sunrise in a long time. I inhaled the morning dew, welcomed all that would come with it.

I had no choice.

The initial itch started on my face. I tensed and started to tingle all over. The burning sensation followed and all I could do was lay there and sizzle, bubble like a salted snail.

I screamed. I fried some more, just like an egg in a skillet.

I screamed like never before. I baked. My flesh smoked, stank, all day. When night came I slept, only to be awakened by another wonderful sunrise that colored the horizon.

So many beautiful hues.

Blood tears ran from my eyes then evaporated as my body started to cook all over again.

Heaven did not exist, but hell did. Something inside of me spoke. *You can give into us and we'll take the pain away.*

Ah, the lunatics that exist in me.

Let go, Kheyang.

I did, and lost consciousness.

Know Thyself

We sabotage ourselves. Then wonder how we fail.

- Cain

We must keep him away, croaked a voice.

But how? He is strong. Our only break is he doesn't know his power.

Time, we need more time.

The treacherous voices in Cain's head only made his dreams more confusing. Images of the woman he once loved, blended with dark halls, coffins and graveyards. One face after another, starting with his father's, and people he didn't recognize, flashed before him.

Eerie, squeaking sounds, clicking, and flapping erupted. A shovel stabbed the earth, followed by the *Shch* from the soil that jerked from the tool, and the solid thud of it hitting the ground.

"My boyaa," Cain heard his mother's sweet voice. "Boyaa, where ya been?" He saw a look of concern. She gave a forced smile. Then she was gone.

There were grunts. Someone strained. Cain had a far away sense it was him. He felt pressure but couldn't place it. He heard the sound of something large being dragged. He saw a blurry bright light, only to go blind by a brighter flash. Smells tickled his nostrils. Cain heard himself chuckle.

Indiscernible chatter berated him. He moaned. A funny taste invaded his mouth. His teeth clicked together. More talking in his mind. *Does he know what we're doing?*

They had complete control, and they were toiling. So in Cain's dreams he felt a sense of work being completed. Something lay in his hands. Something he caressed, and carved, grinded to perfect size.

Darkness again. But he could hear something as it was ripped apart. Maybe a heavy carpet. Cain thought he felt something funny between his fingers. He had a distinct feeling he was tugging it, tearing at the thing. Stickiness. Sadistic dealings.

Again Cain tasted something. It was chewy, slimy, raw. He instinctively grimaced, smacked his lips. The dream world around him had a flurry of bright colors, dull trees, dying grass, moonlight. Wolves wandered at bay. Fog blanketed him at times. The starlit sky sparkled. Graves flirted with him. Music soothed him. Strange melodies played in his head, lyrics of love and hate. Heaving, Cain vomited on himself.

For twenty-seven days Cain drifted between dreams and the real world, gagging, and throwing up all over himself as he lay sprawled in one of the halls of the church.

When he woke and shifted, bolts of pain rippled through him. He cursed.

Stop being so weak, a voice in his mind barked.

"What have you been eating?" Cain ran a hand over his face, wiping away vomit and slime.

Eye balls, chirped the voice. *From the wolves. We killed more of them. And we've been eating for weeks.*

"I thought I was dreaming that," Cain groaned, sitting against a wall. He looked around. It was dark, and he sensed nighttime. "Where am I?"

On the third floor.

"What am I doing here?"

There was no answer, only a moment of uncomfortable silence. Always there was at least a smart remark. But not now. Cain didn't trust them. He realized something hung around his neck.

We made it from the wolves, a voice echoed in his head.

Cain hated the voices. It was impossible at times to discern if they were real, or his own thoughts. He knew that if he wasn't careful they'd take over. They certainly intended to.

Removing the necklace, it rattled. It was made from long, sharp, and polished teeth, and pieces of filed bone that made up the intricate jewelry. Some of the bone still had sinew attached. Others were painted glossy red, green, or black. A few were left in their original color.

In all, it was a morbid necklace and Cain liked it, replacing the trophy around his neck.

Another voice came to life in his head as he stood: *A little longer and we could have kept you from ever coming back.*

Yeah, one whining voice encouraged. *And we know things.*

Shut up, you fool. Are you trying to ruin us?

"What sort of things?" Cain questioned, coming to a flight of stairs.

We've found books. We know the people of this time. Mr. Whining again.

"Impressive. You can read," Cain mocked.

See, he thinks little of us. We'll teach him.

Cain laughed. "You'll go now. That's what you'll do."

Will not. The voice was defiant, and filled Cain's head.

"Leave me!" Cain retaliated with a bellow in a reverberation of voices, and his mind went still.

The great cry in such a dark, lovely church was odd. But the silence absorbed it once again, and the creepiness abounded quite nicely, Cain pondered.

Making his way to the ground floor, the closer Cain came to the stairs that lead below, the more prevalent the peculiar scent became. He started negotiating the steps.

It wasn't the first time he smelled this.

He traversed a corridor, and the stone floor and wall soon gave way to an earth tunnel. It winded on into the darkness.

The smell of rotten egg filled his nostrils. He figured there would be time to explore later, and turned around. Looking over his shoulder one last time, he sensed he had been here before.

Pushing down the corridor that led to his chamber, he was curious as to the new scent that permeated from there. Finally, he saw light dancing at the entrance of his space. The torches in their mounts were lit.

He grunted as he nearly tripped over his feet while he rushed into his lair hunched over, drooling, and with the crazed look of a madman. The nine men he'd killed lay scattered like littered trash, faces and eyes still fashioned in the final moments of struggle and death. Limbs were cast aside. Only Serena's body was laid in some form of humanness. She was on her back with arms folded over her chest. And there was something new in the room. Six mud-caked coffins sat in a semi-circle around his sarcophagus, facing the entrance.

A half-grin caressed Cain's face. The voices, when they took over, had indeed been hard at work. This was good.

Cain's demeanor darkened. What was to be the end to their evil doings? he wondered, realizing he no longer knew himself.

The joints in one coffin creaked as he lifted the top. Inside was a carefully wrapped body from head to toe. Looking upon it, Cain brushed the back of his hand over the side of its face then placed a palm on its stiff chest. "Yes." Cain's head fell back, savoring the sweet feel of the dead.

Satisfied, after viewing each new friend and guardian, he tucked himself into his own coffin, sealing the top. All the bodies were mummified, which to Cain, was that much more alluring. But what was mysterious was that hidden beneath each body in a special compartment, lay a large container that held the corpses' internal organs. Cain marveled.

With a sigh of relief he lay back, closing his eyes (the other was beginning to open and he could half see out of it), and a voice in his head spoke. *There is a special room at the top of the church. Just beyond the third floor. It sits alone and is spacious. A luxurious retreat that rises even higher than the towers.*

Scarlet drapes hang from long rectangular windows giving a panoramic view of the acres that make up the estate.

"What else do you have for me?" Cain muttered, suspicious.

There are secret halls and rooms between the walls.

"What else?"

A pause. *You discovered the caves?*

"Yes. Is there more?"

Bats. There are bats in the caves. Hundreds of beautiful bats.

"What else?"

Another pause. *We intend to destroy you, wiping out your part of us,* the voice pouted.

"What else?"

We plot, and are making arrangements. Special arrangements. The voice was defiant.

"Anything more?"

Nothing worth note.

For two years Cain slept, healing, at least, in part. Yet he remained hideous.

Blood in the Air

Drowsy when I woke, it was like I hadn't rested at all. I felt absolutely depleted.

After every sunset, before digging in the graveyard, I made a habit of hobbling to the start of the woods facing the front of the church. Always too much of a coward to venture further, I peered inward, dreaming of life beyond my estate. However, one evening while taking a deep breath, wonderful smells stimulated my taste buds.

Daring, driven, I took a courageous step further than normal, peeking between the trees. Life was beginning to stir with the sun's departure. It warmed my soul to know I was not the only one hiding from the light.

Taking another step, having not much trouble with my left leg, I grew confident. Like an animal I spied by sniffing the air. Something sweet flirted with my senses.

I could smell human blood. Why did it excite me so?

Losing control, I ventured for the first time ever into the woods, into the exciting unknown.

Bat Dung

Dark cave entrances dotted the wooded hillside a few miles east of the church. Cain stood below at the bank of a half-frozen pond. Sparse blankets of snow covered trees and ground. It was twenty degrees, yet Cain's naked body endured the cold with no adverse effects.

Staring at the cave, his brown eyes went totally black. "Come to me," he whispered. But there was nothing. "Come," he repeated, this time in a chorus of male and female voices that seemed to carry in the wind.

Eerie squeaks echoed, then the rapid sound of leathery wings reverberated in the tiny canyon. For a single moment all the noise stopped. Then hundreds of black-brown bats leapt from the gaping dark and foreboding cave outlets.

Thousands of them! All in that awkward zigzag pattern of flight, and in perfect, unrehearsed precision. There were so many of them the shimmering quarter moon was completely blotted out.

With admiration Cain watched the beautiful movements of the creatures, knowing they were dancing for him. He extended his arms as if to embrace them and they whizzed by in a wild flurry. Cain absorbed their energy, loved their smells and brisk, brutal touch as they flapped by with leathery wings and tiny bodies.

Into the heavens they shot, and down again to engulf the master. To obey. To protect. They swarmed about him like a hive of bees and Cain spun, welcoming them.

Giving a wry grin, Cain knew they would alert him to any trespasser who entered the caves that led to the catacombs beneath the church. They would attack with their razor sharp teeth and claws. They were his to command. They were his friends. His acolytes.

He shouted, "Children!" For they were his children. And he needed children desperately.

A distant, hungry howl interrupted his fixation. Cain looked in that direction. His eyes no longer black, but brown. Lackluster. He was tired of the conflict with the wolves. He wanted a truce, but for some reason they weren't willing.

Patience, he told himself. They would soon be part of his family too. But for now he would have to be satisfied with the little winged, furry rats as kin. Thousands of them, with their sulfuric poop.

Wolves appeared over the hill. Three, then two more. There would be a scrimmage. *Eyeballs. Don't forget to eat the eyeballs,* the voices in Cain's head stirred.

He touched the necklace around his neck. Maybe he'd add a few claws.

Dancing

Done digging and arranging the coffins below, reading became Cain's favorite pastime. Mostly he was attracted to stories about ancient civilizations. The ones in particular that reminded him of his own were North and South American Indian cultures. Or the great Kemetian nation prior to the Egyptians. He disliked reads on conquerors the most. Unfortunately they seemed to fill volumes, but he read them anyway. He wanted to know as much as he could of the world around him. And in so doing, he uncovered many of his own people's finger prints.

The Unspoken Order seemed to have been obsessed with collecting artifacts. They filled many of the rooms of the church while the upper rooms were mostly bare, or if not, carried merely books and scrolls. Especially the four towers that jutted from the church like mountain peaks.

Often, as he read, he'd listen to a record. Nat King Cole had become his favorite. The song, "My Funny Valentine," by Miles Davis was a close runner-up.

The mausoleum's marble floors reflected the moon's light with contemplative beauty. For days at a time Cain would walk the halls of the tiny burial place talking to the encapsulated bodies. He had a sense that they could hear and understand him.

With every pressing day Cain's boldness to venture into the woods became greater, and he went deeper. Incidentally, clashes with wolves became fewer. Yet they were still seen trotting across the estate in search of food, seemingly unafraid. From a window in one of the upper stories of the church Cain would peer at the beasts. He could relate to their insatiable hunger. Every fiber of his body called out for food. But no matter what he ate, it did not satisfy his needs for nourishment. He was perplexed.

He was famished.

"Unforgettable, that's what you are," Cain sang along with Nat in a carpeted bedroom. He paced back and forth, and in his imagination he whispered the words to his love in her ear as they embraced, dancing.

He was healed, his old, strong, whole self. As always his woman was vibrant, giggling, happy.

"My Funny Valentine. Please don't change a thing for me," he now whispered as he nibbled her ear. In his mind they waltzed alone in the palatial church. They swayed until the music stopped and Cain was once again utterly alone in a decaying eighteenth century structure with a Spanish-Moor design. A place where a mausoleum and a dark, dark catacomb was his only solace in a world that didn't seem to know he existed

All that, he was determined, would somehow change.

Happier Times

"I love ya, Kheyang."

"Ya ar me heart, woman," Kheyang swore, pounding a fist upon his chest to emphasize his words. He got the response he was looking for when she gave that sunlight, shy smile of hers.

"Why don't ya walk wit me today?"

"Woman, ya no I must work. Ya no dhis."

"Ya always work'n," she pouted.

Kheyang stopped, ran a finger along her face to move the thick hanging dreadlocks. He lusted as he stared at her naked flesh.

"For I," she pleaded. Seeing the look of surrender in his eyes, she quickly took advantage by saying, "Good, catch I if ya kin, Kheyang," and shot through the thick vegetation.

Kheyang gladly gave chase but she was a swift girl. Faster than the many jack rabbits he'd hunted. His woman giggled as she looked over her shoulder, never breaking her stride.

The way her buttocks bounced as she ran stirred Kheyang's loins and he pushed much harder to catch her. Again she looked back, teasing, then hurled herself through more bush, dashing between fruit trees.

Just as he thought he would reach out and grab her she turned swiftly and leapt over the cliff-side that they had been running parallel to. Shocked, Kheyang called out for her and stood at the edge just in time to watch her splash into a large pool of water below.

"Damn ya, woman!" he shouted. He had feared the worst and hated heights.

She laughed, crawled onto the bank and flopped onto her back, mocking Kheyang. He frowned, gave a curse. Then, attempting to show courage though his heart pumped with fear, he jumped.

His locks flailed. His insides pushed up into his throat from the weightlessness. It took forever for him to splash into the water, where he kicked and paddled like any poor swimmer.

Oh, how the woman laughed. Kheyang was swallowing more water than he treaded, and just before he reached dry land she took off. Not as if he really had enough wind to pursue. He lay sprawled on his back gasping for air.

The woman surprised him by hopping on top of him and pushing his back flat against the mud. She leaned down and kissed his lips under the bright sky. His hands automatically grabbed her formidable hind end, spreading it apart, but she sprung to her feet.

"Oh Kheyang. Ya neva gone catch I lay'n dhere on ya back like a likkle gal." She licked her lips and shot off.

"I gone git ya in teach ya who da likkle gal!" he threatened as he stood.

"Over ere, Kheyang!" she shouted; and he turned in her voice's direction but she was gone. "No, I over ere, Kheyang," she called from another position.

She was using the great power of muddah that he taught her. So to even the game he called upon the same force, and when his woman called from another place and turned with a giggle to flee, she ran into Kheyang's strong arms.

"Now what ya gone do, woman?" he breathed, holding her tight.

"Surrendah." She kissed him and he gently pulled her to the ground.

The contrast of their bodies, his dark reddish brown skin, her fair wonderful complexion, was a perfect blend. Kheyang pushed his throbbing flesh into her pink softness and moved inside her. He marveled at how well her inner walls seemed to tug on his hardness. She ran her tongue hungrily over his nipples, nibbling, biting. He pinned her against the earth, gently cupping her head with one hand while holding one of her legs over his shoulder so he could slide deeper into her core.

She moaned with pleasure and as he continued to plunge deep, her body trembled. Kheyang felt warm slippery fluids saturate his groin and continued to gyrate, thoroughly blending their juices. At one point he didn't think he'd ever stop fucking her. Even though he pumped cum into her body his shaft stayed hard as iron. He couldn't get enough of the woman.

Cain woke to a stone hard dick but his only desire was to kill. He pushed aside the cover to his coffin and crawled out. The grey tint of his eyes had tiny threads of red veins running through them. There was a single thump of his heart. Still, his flesh was cold as ice, although nowhere near as icy as his soul had become.

Laying back, all he could think of was the day they made love under the sun with not a care in the world. It was that day he was sure she had conceived their child.

Hunger Pangs

I was ashamed as I looked at my naked body in a long mirror. What was I? In rage I struck the glass, shattering it and cutting my hand. I squeezed my fist and thick blood oozed briefly between my fingers.

As soon as the sun dropped below the horizon, I burst through the doors of the church donned in black, loose-fit clothing. Once I reached the trees I stopped and inhaled the life of the forest before taking off in a burst of speed.

Trees and brush whizzed by. Even with an injured leg my stride was long and consistent. I broke no sweat, barely breathed at all. I was moving three or four times the speed of the average human and I knew from experience that I could only keep up this pace for so long, and that I'd pay dearly afterwards. Using up my energy often left me writhing in pain. But something, a lust that was far from sexual, tugged at me, urged me to push harder, faster. It was a primal, frightening desire. One that I did not understand, but wanted to satisfy.

After a mere few hours I was outside a small town. But I dared not enter, and only lurked on the outskirts like some depraved beast. Watching, wanting. But what, what did I want? Why was I watching?

Just watching, a voice in my head whispered.

It was a cloudless evening with no moon, but stars were out in full. My vision was strong enough to where I could see a mouse scrounging about for food near one sidewalk trash can.

People were out. Some just strolled, occasionally looking through the window of one of the closed shops. I wanted to join in the window shopping. But in a strange way I felt that window shopping was exactly what I was doing.

From my perch I could hear conversations a mile away. People driving by in cars, walking, it did not matter. I was spying on all of them with success. Everyone seemed happy and full of life. While I suffered, slinking in the shadows like a wraith.

With anger and envy I leapt from the tree and made for the church. With each step fury grew inside of me. My flesh was cold and clammy. I felt weak and my strength waned. Before I could slow down I lost my footing, tripped and fell face first, taking in a mouth full of soil and leaves. Rolling onto my back, pain strangled my gut. It felt as if I were starving to death. But I had not the slightest taste for food.

I staggered to my feet, my wounded leg heavy like stone. Dizziness threatened to send me to the ground again where I didn't think I'd find the power to get up. Yet somehow I managed to drag my leg along yard after difficult yard.

Hours went by and my body was stiff and ached. My left shoe had worn through from dragging my mangled leg. The church, the church was all I could think of.

"Please, no," I gasped, when I saw the first thread of light in the distance.

Pangs in my stomach flared, sending me to my knees. I lowered my head and wept. I knew I would receive a lashing, a reward for leaving my only sanctuary.

When I raised my head the rays of the sun greeted me. They showered me gently and I extended my arms to feel the warmth. I threw back my head, closing my eyes, waiting. At first there was a tingling sensation all over. Then came the hell-fire, and I screamed, knowing there was no one to help me.

Trapped in an inferno, I collapsed to the ground, balled like a helpless infant. I rocked, moaned from the hunger that had my stomach spasming, wrenching in knots. My skin started to smolder and my clothing caught ablaze. I scrambled to get it off my body.

To the church, get to the church, the voices in my head pressed. That was all I heard as I clawed my way across the earth until finally I was upon the stone doorsteps. Still, getting inside seemed to take an eternity. Darkness came over me as I lay on the floor of the church like a piece of burnt charcoal, for weeks.

The Old Woman

A hideous, menacing cackle awakened Cain. His seared flesh stank and his stomach roiled. He pushed himself to his knees and grimaced in agony but he was no stranger to pain.

The front doors of the church were flung open. It was night fall and a cool breeze blew in. Cain went to the porch. Folds of fog drifting by, he strained to see between them into the darkness. The air he inhaled was clean, no one was about... Except... he sensed a woman. An old woman. She was staring at him from out there somewhere. She was not afraid of him.

"Show yourself!" Cain called, stepping off the porch. The fog swirled around him as he passed. "I know you're watching! You watch me even in the church. You are daring to trespass. Do you find me amusing?" He did not like the idea of this person coming into his domain, into his very chamber, uninvited. Waiting. Watching.

Maybe even manipulating him.

"What are you waiting for?" A woman's hoarse voice cut through the dark, foggy distance. Cain made out the vague outline of a figure.

"A ghost?" he replied off-handed.

A coarse, almost masculine laugh followed. "You don't believe in ghosts ... or has your heart changed?"

"What do you know of my heart?"

"Enough. Or perhaps hardly anything. As much as you."

The fog thickened, swallowing the woman's image. Yet Cain knew she was still there. "What are you waiting for?" she taunted again.

"And that means?"

"You don't want to play with me, young man." It was a stern response. One that prompted Cain to walk down the dirt road that winded from the church.

Once the road came to the woods it wound north-east. But the coarse whisper of the woman called from the north-west, off the road and in a direction Cain had never explored.

"Keep coming. That's it. That's it." Her voice carried in the night.

"Who are you?" Cain asked.

Hissing wafted, and more laughter. "Who would you like me to be?"

Cain pushed deeper, with the brush becoming thick and tangled.

"Riddles. Why?"

"Because you don't want the truth."

Just as Cain started having real difficulty maneuvering through the woods they loosened into a clearing, where only twenty yards away stood a person, bundled, and hunched, facing the opposite direction .

Cain stopped. The slightest hint of cinnamon tickled his nostrils. "Who are you, old woman?"

"Everything you aren't, or want to be. Everything you were, and are." She paused. Then her voice cracked, as she continued. "Who I am doesn't matter as much as what we mean to each other." She sounded much older than before, weaker. She sounded like a woman who had many fantastic tales she could share. She wheezed.

Cain rounded her position but she moved with him, keeping her back to him.

"Are we the same?" Cain questioned.

Chortling again. "Hardly."

"You aren't human."

"Neither are you." Her head tilted. "Not human at all." It slipped from her tongue like poison.

Recalling a conversation between Duvall and William that he'd spied on with his senses, Cain said, "You are the witch."

"The witch," she parroted. "I suppose I am - the witch." Her tone had a conniving quality to it.

"You want me to search for my father. Like the others did."

"Do I?"

"Of course you do. But he's dead."

"So sure? Yet you live."

"Something evil happened to me. Perhaps a curse for killing my brother and rising against my father."

"Cursed, you say," she chuckled. Cain hated that she mocked him with every remark.

"What do you want with me?" he growled.

"Hmm, darling. There is room for mutual benefit here."

Now Cain laughed heartily. "No, I don't trust one as sly as you." He closed within a few feet of her. Her tattered, worn clothing was in no better condition than his half burned, and filthy garbs.

"You don't trust me. How ironic, for if you don't, you will die."

"Threatening me?" Cain retaliated.

Her shoulders rolled as she laughed. The cinnamon scent grew stronger.

"I have grown beyond threatening. Power needn't threaten. By definition it does so itself."

"So, why am I in danger?"

"Because you have been found. Because even as weak as you are, you grow stronger. Because your power emits like a beacon. You must sleep more until it is time."

"Sleep...I do so often."

"No, you must go deeper. Deeper even than you did when buried. It must be undisturbed. You must have no thoughts, no feelings. You must sleep as if dead."

He rolled her words in his mind. "Why must I do this? And until it is time for what?"

"I am not your teacher."

"Yet you are full of instruction."

"Quick at the tongue. Cute. Dangerous ... I told you that there is mutual benefit in this. That is why I am here."

Cain placed a hand on her shoulder and pulled. She turned. To his surprise, a young, beautiful and exotic woman presented herself beneath the layers of old black rags. Her eyes were wide and brown, her lips, succulent. She grinned and stood erect. Her teeth were perfect white pearls.

Cain removed her hood, and long silver hair contrasted her youthfulness and brown skin. "Where do you come from?"

"From very far away. Like you." She stepped closer and stood on her toes to whisper in his ear. She encouraged him to, "Explore beyond the woods." Then she stepped off.

Heading away, the woman stopped and turned, giving a flirtatious wink. "And sleep more. Much more. And deeply."

"Your name?" Cain asked.

"Helena."

The fog engulfed the witch, and she was gone.

Gratification

Seven years later, 1978: Sleep I did, and deeper than I ever had before. It somewhat healed me. But more than that, left me feeling powerful. Yet still I could not manifest this power…It eluded me.

A breeze swept over me, colder than the blood in my veins, and I knew a storm was coming. Clouds gathered and I grew excited knowing the rain would invigorate me.

While I stood on one of the balconies of the church, the wind blew fierce, howling and whipping about as if angry. I knew the exact moment the droplets would start, so I allowed my head to fall back as I outstretched my arms, closing my eyes to enjoy the sensations that pelted me. It was wonderful.

A bold idea came to mind. Now I could roam the streets of a city I knew south of here. Closer than the town that had taught me a lesson. It wasn't too late and I could make it back in time before sunrise if I didn't exert myself. But it was late and rainy enough to ensure I'd have the streets to myself.

Thrilled, I threw on a long trench coat and headed out for what I hoped to be a delightful evening in the city.

It was close to midnight when I reached my destination and the rain had stopped, though dark clouds remained in a tight bundle above. The air was sweet, the water having cleansed everything. The atmosphere was inviting.

Casually strolling down one street I peered into a closed store window imagining myself interacting with a clerk inside. Maybe to buy, or just try something on. I yearned desperately for human interaction.

Drizzle teased me. Lightening erupted across the sky. I could hardly wait for the rainfall again. It was addictive and it was my insurance for cover.

Adrift in my own thoughts, that familiar throb in my temples caught my attention. Someone was close. Before I could react a man and woman locked in each others arms turned a corner and strode right past me. I pulled my cap further down to hide myself and grunted, clutching my head. The sharp metallic shrill was deafening as if someone had dropped a sharp cleaver in the center of my forehead.

The couple never paid me any mind, even when I leaned against the building to keep my distance as they passed. But once they were gone I knew it was time for me to head back to the church not only to beat the sunrise, but to avoid pushing my luck.

Just as I decided to vacate, I heard heels tapping on the sidewalk across the slick street. The woman wore a coat and carried an umbrella. She was oblivious to my presence. Yet I noticed her, thoroughly. Would have even if my eyes hadn't, and not only because of the throbbing in my temples that tortured me. Her perfume, the fragrance, drew me in.

But the pain she caused me. I hated her for that and the desire to make her pay burned in my chest.

Make her pay, make her pay. Make her suffer for the life force screeching through her body.

I followed at a discreet distance. Through a small park she led me down a cement path, never aware I was gaining ground. Trees lined our route. The wind blew harder. Still the woman had not noticed that I, the predator, was nearly upon her. The pounding in my head was the price, but my reward would be worth it. Her steps were brisk but she'd never make it to her destination. She didn't know I had the power to stop her from reaching her course, and I marveled in the thought.

Something unusual started to take place; my heart beat stronger, and in sync with hers. I felt veins bulging in my forehead and neck. All rational thinking was gone from me. All I knew was that I would kill her.

Around the bend darkness enveloped us. I was so close…I reached out to take her by the shoulders but a man came our way.

I fell back with great speed. Something made her look over her shoulder, but I was gone. The man passed her and turned, pulling out a knife. Rain started to fall heavy. Anger rushed over me at the thought of his impudence. *How dare he interfere with my kill?!*

Before thinking I leapt and in one motion battered him in the back. He went hard to the ground, spun around and scrambled to his feet. I stepped forward. He thrust the blade in my stomach. I accepted the strike and returned the favor with a solid fist to his ribs that lifted him into the air.

Withdrawing the knife, tossing it to the side, I was upon him before he could find his bearing. I took great pleasure in inflicting pain with my bare hands. His bones cracked without resistance beneath my royal feet. I was Kheyang.

Of course I was better than he. Father was right. *I am better than them*, ran through my thoughts. But did I really feel that way? Something had taken control.

His heart, which pounded heavily at the initial assault, now beat very slowly, in perfect unison with mine. For some reason the woman was now of no consequence. Oblivious to her near death, she was making her way home.

With disgust I looked upon the man. I knew he was nothing. Less than the grit beneath my shoes. My head throbbed because of this jackal and I knew how to make it stop. I would make it stop.

But for some reason I hesitated. My nostrils flared. I wiped the corners of my mouth with a sleeve. I was salivating.

I looked around. The park was deserted. I threw his limp body over my shoulders and headed for the church. I was surprised how easy it was. The thought of taking his life gave me energy. I hoped it would last.

There was a chance that if the sun rose the dark clouds would protect me. With each muddy step through the woods I told myself, *I can do this, I can do this*. I repeated it aloud again and again until it became a chant. Then the voices in my head cheered me on, propelling me forward. Some oddly sang a happy tune. We were all in this together. I salivated the whole way.

He was unconscious. His heart beat was steady and I looked upon him with hate. So much life in his veins pained me physically, and filled me with jealousy.

What was I going to do with him now? To him? Unconsciously licking my lips, I mused. I'd read vampire tales about how they drank the blood of their human prey. Could those stories be about me? I ran my fingers along my teeth. They were smooth, uniform, no sharp canines.

Suddenly the pain in my head increased as the man regained consciousness. I staggered back when his eyes popped open. My image sent him into a wild frenzy. He was bound by ropes to a bed yet he struggled to break free, grimacing from broken ribs. He coughed, gagged, and spat out bright red beautiful blood. So wonderful was it that I could hardly take my eyes off it.

I mocked him with a laugh as I watched him struggle to free himself to no avail. He leaned away from me and I knew why. The stench from my breath made him sick. Despite having all my teeth, my gums were black and rotten.

Fear had his blood pumping, pushing very fast through his arteries. I grabbed my head and groaned. Then I flashed him a wild look and stepped forward. I reached out and slapped him hard with a back hand. The strike released tension, although it did nothing to relieve the pressure in my head.

Rushing to the restroom, I downed a handful of pain pills with cold water from the sink then threw water on my face. I kept my head down, afraid to look at myself in the mirror. But after a while the temptation was too great and to my own regret, I lifted my head to my reflection. I gasped in horror at the sight. My eyes were lifeless black holes, sunken, shriveled to nothing, surrounded by dark, deep circles. My skin was grey with white blotches of clear liquid secreting like slime. I looked away. But there was that constant painful thump of his heart to vex me. This had to stop, and I rushed down a long unlit corridor to the kitchen. Looking around the cobwebbed room, I snatched open a drawer and withdrew a sharp knife. Then I stormed back to the bedroom. The terror filled his blue eyes when he saw the steak knife. I yielded. I did not want to kill this creature with it. I needed to experiment. So I slashed his wrist and he howled like a kicked dog.

His cries and begging meant nothing to me. The blood that ran from his wrist had my full attention. It was so red and thick. My lips naturally parted, I licked them. I was fixated on his blood.

I kneeled beside him, he twisted in vain. I licked his wrist and my body spasmed with violence. My heart jumped for the first time in thousands of years.

I sucked on the slit across his wrist, the rich warm substance tasted like the most exotic delicacy. I stood and stepped away from him repulsed. As I rose, I wiped my mouth and looked at my hand. It swelled and color showed. I closed and opened my fist, feeling the power. The pain in my head subsided. But the hunger intensified. All I could do was laugh heartily. The vampire stories had truth in them.

I laughed again and fell upon my victim's neck, biting away flesh with my dull teeth. The screams from him only excited and provoked me to suck the fluids that squirted from his throat with more tenacity. I stopped only when not a drop was left.

Home Sweet Home

Do ya love I?"

"What kind of question dhat, woman?" Kheyang responded by throwing an arm around her waist and pulling her closer as they walked. He kissed her neck and she giggled.

"Have ya been wit adhers?" she asked shyly, pulling away from him.

They stopped walking; chirping birds danced in the bristling tree tops around them while small animals scurried about below.

He lifted his chin, contemplating. "I have been wit many adheres." He knew the words stung. She looked away and stepped back. "But none I love," he added.

"None of dhem, Kheyang?" she asked in a broken voice.

Kheyang realized how much pain he had inflicted with his truthful answer. "None," he muttered, watching her tears flow.

"Dhen why?" She faced him bravely.

"Ya love none of dhem, Kheyang?" his twin brother Ablah interrupted, stepping out from behind a tree with a sinister grin. His eyes fell upon the woman and gave her a lascivious glance. He sucked in his breath and popped his lips.

"What ya want, Ablah?" Kheyang's mood soured. He balled his fist.

"Not I, Kheyang," Ablah stood behind Kheyang's woman, placing hands on her shoulder. He felt her distress. "Domm, a faddah called," Ablah corrected. Being so close to the girl, his dick stirred and swelled against her.

"Woman, I will come fa ya." Kheyang pulled her away from his brother.

Ablah chuckled, amused at his brother's defensiveness.

Wanting to argue, but seeing the seriousness in Kheyang's eyes, she huffed and asked, "When, Kheyang?" Her eyes averted Ablah's, which were making her uncomfortable.

"Me told ya woman, I will come. Now find ya self gone," he answered with force.

It was enough that she jumped with fear, turned and ran off. Ablah was shrewd enough that he watched her bouncing body parts with a gleam that unsettled Kheyang.

"Da woman seem sweet like wild honey, Kheyang." Ablah's dick stood straight out.

Immediately Kheyang shoved him against a tree and warned, "Leave dhat girl be, Ablah. A ya gone git big trouble."

Ablah smirked and threw his brother's hands off. He then shrugged and headed away. Kheyang seethed with anger but followed without a word.

Cain's eyes opened to darkness. He boiled with hatred that went back thousands of years. He closed his eyes again and immediately slept.

"Faddah," Ablah greeted as he and his brother approached.

Domm placed a firm hand on Kheyang's shoulder. Kheyang responded in kind. It was a warm, affectionate formality. Domm smiled at Kheyang then grunted at Ablah who immediately took his cue and retreated. In silence he led his son through a beautiful garden. Attendees were sure to keep busy and out of their way as they passed.

"Why do dhey act so sheepish, faddah?" Kheyang asked as he observed the humans.

Domm didn't answer but sat on a large half buried boulder. Next to him was an orange tree. He picked one of the low hanging fruits and peeled the bright colored thick husk.

"Son I will tell ya all ya need to no bout every ting. Da kind, da kindred, our history. Ya future, boyaa." He looked at his son with pride as he chewed on the sweet fruit.

"Of home?" Kheyang was curious.

Domm smiled. "Bout it all." He looked into the rich blue sky. But his thoughts seemed to be far past the atmosphere above. Kheyang figured they were many millions of miles away.

Again Cain woke, but this time sorrow, not anger, filled him. His father never got the chance to tell him what he wanted him to know because things between them changed forever.

Closing his eyes again, he dreamt: As a boy he stumbled drowsily down a strange corridor. The lighting was dim, it was quiet. Rubbing his watery eyes he continued down another hall, and towards voices...

Leaning against the entrance to a room, he peered in. His dreadlocks were past his waist, and he had to continue pulling them out of his eyes.

Two of the men in conversation were white and also had dreadlocks, very thick, shoulder length and blonde. The third adult was the one the boy recognized as his father, Domm.

"We not gone wake the brethren and sistern," one man angrily debated.

Domm said, "Dhem our kin."

"But dhis also our last chance. We gone have ta tink of ourselves, Domm." The third, and oldest of the three stated, "Fa now we gone let dhem sleep. Da adhers, we not gone call." His voice was steady, smooth. He was tall, thin, and had the bluest eyes. There was something about the way they seemed to absorb the light in the room.

Domm beat his fist against the table. "Don't ya two forget. I one have da powah. En me powah biggah din both yas together."

The room grew quiet. Domm heard the boy stir and turned. "Kheyang, me first born. Ya spying on ya faddah." He grinned. "Shoo boyaa, git," he fanned.

One final time Cain woke. However this time he slid the cover away and stepped from his crypt. He wore dark clothing. The color of his skin was rich brown. He had eyebrows and eye lashes, and deep brown eyes. Very thick dreadlocks flowed in a long ponytail that hung below his waist. Cain was completely healed. His heart beat was steady and pumped warm blood through his veins.

It was the feeding that had revived him. He figured this was what the Unspoken Order meant about revitalization. Cain could and did travel under the light of the sun with no burning sensation. He could enjoy the warmth as it beat down on his face like any normal man. Except that he felt more alive than an average man and had an eternity to experience life. Cain also discovered that when he was flush with new blood he could interact with humans and not experience the migraines or ear-screeching metallic shrill of their blood rushing through their veins. He was free and able to move about as he wished. No one suspected what he was. He wasn't sure himself.

There are degrees of love. But the highest degree is so great it changes your life for the better, forever. It is a place that will live and light the heart in the darkest of times. It will never leave you alone.

-Kheyang

Sacred Faith

April 23, 2003

It was Cain's first train experience and his first time traveling across the state of Virginia where he lived. It was daring, he had no destination. He didn't know why he had such a strong desire to travel. He just knew he had to get away from the church and that ever lurking witch for a little while. She had unclear motives, and Cain did not trust her. In addition, he grew weary of the deep sleeping.

Taking a window seat, he spied the people around him as inconspicuously as possible. *Who could be a vampire?* he wondered. *Will I be able to recognize one?* He hoped so. He was tired of being alone.

When he wasn't reviewing faces he busied himself on a laptop researching vampires. Trying to figure out fact from fiction was frustrating. He only had himself as a reference, and considered himself a bad one at that.

Once tired of the Internet, he stared out the window at the ever-changing scenery until his mind went far from everything around him. At times like this he'd enter a place no one else could go, a place in his heart where he loved a woman who loved him back.

Cain was desperately alone.

When the train stopped at another station, an old gentleman boarded and sat directly in front of Cain. Sighing as he sat, he acknowledged Cain with a smile. Cain returned the gesture then immediately looked out the window to suggest he did not want any conversation.

The man across from him noticed and pulled out a Bible to read. That was when Cain realized the man wore a black suit with a cross and a distinct white collar.

First Father

A woman behind the minister, sneezed. "God bless you," the priest remarked and the woman thanked him.

Cain was tickled at the exchange and it obviously showed on his face because the minister leaned forward and said to him, "I don't really know why we say it either. Why not when a person coughs too? Or passes gas? Though in that regard, I can't imagine anyone blessing someone because of flatulence."

Cain chuckled; there was something about the man that he immediately warmed to.

"I have a genuine question..." Cain started.

The old man leaned back and gave him a frank look. "Well, I will give you a genuine answer, young man."

Cain marveled at the remark, realizing he did appear to be young...about thirty five. "Do you really believe in that book?" He nodded toward the Bible in his lap.

The priest stared at him with narrowed eyes for a long time, as if trying to figure him out, then finally said, "It is the word of God. I believe every word of it."

Cain had a better time reading into him. Through his eyes he traveled deep into his soul, and sensed contradiction. The minister felt uncomfortable and shifted. He then pulled a handkerchief from a pocket and dabbed his forehead to wipe away tiny beads of sweat.

"I see," Cain replied stoically. "And what if there were no *word of God*, would you still believe in him?" He gestured upward with a grin.

"Yes, I would know in my heart there was a God."

"Would you have the desire to be close to this God?" Cain looked at him intently, watching every blink, every twitch, every uncomfortable shift.

The minister contemplated the question. "I believe I would have a desire to be in that position."

"Which relationship would be greater, the one where you have a book as you do now, or the one where you are forced to have a natural relationship?" Cain sat back. He was reading the

112

man's cluttered mind, already knowing what he was about to say, and lost genuine interest because of it.

"Keep in mind," his companion cleared his throat. "The nature of man is inherently evil and God gave us his word as instruction, because in our natural state we do not know how to live."

With a shrug, Cain responded, "I wonder if you'd give that same answer of man's nature if you had not read it in a book."

The old man smiled warmly. "Faith is a hard thing to have in life, young man. Sometimes it is strong. Other times weak." He paused. "Son-" he touched Cain's hand but withdrew as a cold sensation ran up his spine. He needed a moment to gather himself. "Sometimes on this journey we lose all faith. But you can find it again," he finished.

Without reply Cain stared out the window thinking about "faith". Thinking about all of the things he knew about faith. He knew enough to be certain he did not want any part of it. If anything were inherently evil it was faith. From what his father told him, his people had proven it, and knowledge of that made his kind greater.

At the next stop the priest gathered his belongings, got off the train, and waved down a taxi. Something compelled Cain to pursue, and he called for a taxi too. The pursuit wasn't long, the old man got out of the cab when they reached a large church a few blocks away. From there, Cain ordered his driver to take him to a nice hotel in the area.

Once in his room Cain laid on the floor beside the bed. The solid surface against his back was familiar and soothing but not enough for him to sleep in peace. For thirty four years since his release from the grave he had only found solace when resting in his crypt.

He stared at the ceiling. He couldn't get the priest out of his head. He wanted to go deeper with their conversation. He wanted the truth from the man. No, he knew the truth. He needed the man to admit it. It was the only thing that would get the man out of his head, he figured.

Two young priests did their rounds and locked the chapel before turning in. Unbeknownst to them, Cain had managed to slip inside without detection. He took refuge in the shadowed alcoves, and moved with stealth, too quickly for a human to perceive.

Once sure that everyone was settled, Cain concentrated by closing his eyes. The sound of three separate heartbeats filled his ears. It was like music, inviting him to sup. But he was not hungry, and wasn't here for that. He salivated, and wiped his mouth. He summoned self-control and kept listening until he distinguished the heart he was looking for.

Soundlessly, Cain followed the sound of the rhythmic thump down one hall after another until he reached a closed door. Light seeped from underneath, indicating that the occupant was probably awake.

Leaning against the door, Cain closed his eyes, savoring the precious sound of the man's blood flowing through his veins. He licked his lips. *I'm not hungry*, he reminded himself. Liar. Who was he kidding? There was hunger inside of him.

Curiosity had cast its enchantment. He wanted the truth spoken or demonstrated. He could hear it whisper as it flowed throughout his victim's body. *No*, Cain told himself, *this man is not intended to be a victim. I am here to prove that his actions contradict his heart, his soul.*

Cain could read the man's secret thoughts, knowing he questioned everything. Yes, he knew a like soul when he met one. He knew hurt and disappointment. He could see a trapped man. He knew what pressure on one's shoulder looked like. He knew a lie when he heard it. It had no conviction, and only persecuted one's soul as long as one lived it.

Cain shook his head and clenched his teeth. Upset with himself, he pulled away from the door and turned to see a young priest staring at him. He had been so engrossed in his thoughts that he hadn't paid attention to his instincts warning him of the man's approach.

"Who are -" was all that escaped the man's mouth before Cain was upon him, his eyes red like lava. Before he could gather his thoughts, he covered the man's mouth with his hands and quieted his resistance. Then, ripped into the side of his neck and slurped sloppily. Within moments, Cain felt the weight of a dead man in his arms. The scent of blood was overpowering.

"My God!" shouted a voice. The older priest was joined by a younger colleague who'd apparently heard the commotion. They both raced down the hall.

Cain started after them, but in no particular hurry. They entered a study, and locked and barricaded it by propping a chair against the doorknob.

"Quickly!" The old priest pointed. "There is a gun in that drawer." While the young priest retrieved the pistol, the elder retrieved the box of bullets he kept on the shelf and began dumping them into his hand. "Hurry!"

The younger man's breathing was sporadic and beads of sweat were forming on his brow. He fumbled the revolver, then somehow managed to calm himself and hand it to the older gentleman. Now it was the older priest's turn to be nervous; he dropped a handful of rounds as he shakily loaded the weapon.

A knock sounded at the door. Both men looked at one another.

"We have a weapon, a gun. I suggest you go away," the old priest threatened.

The younger man tore a leg off a wooden chair and tip-toed closer to the door holding the leg like a baseball bat. Cain plowed the door into the man, rendering him unconscious.

The first shot came as Cain stepped inside the room yet it did nothing but jerk his right shoulder as it tore through him. The wound healed instantly, pushing the round out of his flesh so that it fell to the floor with a jingle.

Again the priest fired, this time pointing for Cain's head. The poorly aimed projectile instead ripped through the side of his neck only to quickly heal, hardly slowing the vampire's pace.

He closed his eyes and squeezed the trigger with Cain at point blank range; the bullet blasted through his torso and out the other side. Again Cain healed just as quickly. Then he back-handed the man into the air.

Cain approached, his eyes pitch black. Which at least meant he hadn't intentions to feed, like when red. The old man grappled aimlessly about as he scooted backwards. He searched for a weapon or shield, anything. Somehow he obtained a Bible and held it outward with both hands as if it would ward off Cain's approach. He prayed to God above, pulling his requests from deep within. Cain stopped, quite amused.

"Tell me, priest-" Cain wiped his gore covered face with a sleeve- "is that book you hope will protect you, sacred? Is it holy?" He raised an eyebrow.

"Yes," he answered with no reserve. "Most holy, most sacred."

Cain admired the man's feigned confidence and persistence. "More holy than you?"

"Without question." He backed against a wall.

"More holy than..." Cain toyed with him, looking about. "...than your companion?" He motioned to the unconscious man.

"Of course, yes." He was resolved but cowered under the monster's advance.

Smiling, Cain took a slow step back. Then with incredible speed went over, grabbed, and tossed the unconscious victim at the other man's feet. Cain then claimed the gun and also threw it at the old man's feet. The whole process took less than a second and the speed of it further terrified the priest.

"Follow my instructions to the letter or I will kill you and your associate without reserve," Cain roared.

"What are you?" the man pleaded.

With a shake of the head, he replied, "No different from you where it counts. Now, you have twenty seconds to demonstrate that which is most sacred and holy. You will either put a round into that Bible or his brain." Cain snatched the book out of his hand and threw it to the floor. "That book or his head," he repeated, pointing to each.

The unconscious man's chest raised and lowered at a moderate pace. The Catholic priest reached for the gun. His hand trembled. Cain turned his back and counted down. "Ten seconds, nine…" He paused. "…six, five…"

There was a single gunshot. Cain turned; the Bible had a hole through the center. He leaned and picked it up, looking through the hole at the man.

Cain inhaled deeply, then exhaled and dropped the tome. "In your heart of heart's you know the truth." He looked into the unwavering eyes of the man. "You have always known the truth of that which is holy and sacred.

"Your brother and his blood. Not that book, not its words. But the life pumping through his precious veins." Bending down near him Cain whispered, "But we lie to ourselves, brother." With that, he moved so fast through the exit that it seemed as if he'd vanished into thin air.

The priest wept, not for himself but for his dead friend in the hall whom he believed was no more. There was no purgatory, no heaven, no hell.

No saints or salvation …no God.

Whatever there was, Father Donovan Edmasses would have to find it all over again. His faith was thoroughly broken.

Familiar Face

Back at the hotel, Cain rinsed the blood off in the shower then bathed in a warm bath to enjoy the feel of the water, which relaxed him. Massaging his temples, the image of when he attacked the priest flashed through his mind. He struggled to understand why he'd killed the man. Why did he feed when he wasn't hungry?

The urge to drink from him was instant and absolute once he saw him. Before he could think he had acted. It was frightening, the total loss of control that had swept over him.

It was perplexing because the trigger eluded him. The desire to feed he both hated and loved. Drinking made him feel alive.

He wiped the corners of his salivating mouth with his thumb and forefinger, not realizing for a moment his eyes had slivers of red running through them.

Once done bathing he sat on the bed, grabbed the remote and aimlessly flicked through the channels. He didn't really intend to watch anything, so after awhile he pushed what he thought was the off button. It was yet another channel. Since the volume was muted he had not realized it was still on when he tossed the remote on the bed and started getting dressed.

He slipped on his blue jeans and was reaching for a silk long sleeve buttoned shirt when he noticed the television still on. And more, there was a news clip with a familiar face on the screen.

He grappled for the remote and pressed the mute button just in time to hear, "Parole denied for the third time for Richard Stace, the man who strangled and mutilated Patricia Hartway and Michael Barnes in Roadside Park twenty five years ago. Stace will remain in Leavenworth Penitentiary in Kansas where he is serving a life sentence."

Cain flipped off the TV and pulled out his computer. He googled "Richard Stace," and up popped the same photograph that had attracted Cain's attention. Nothing else was of interest.

That face ... Cain looked through more articles hoping to come across a video of the man talking but found none. He sat back, wishing he could hear the man's voice. He would know for sure then. Or, he mused, he could just visit him.

Visitation

Cain looked about the visiting room in wonder. If the man were truly a vampire, why would he subject himself to this place? *Maybe I'm wrong,* Cain thought, and was about to get up and leave when a very tall, thin man in prison blues entered through a side door unlocked by a frowning guard. His strides were smooth and long. He almost seemed to glide. He was probably in his early seventies but had a youthful appearance. Long silver hair flowed over his shoulders and down to the center of his back. His eyes, though they never seemed to cross Cain's, were alert.

The old man checked in with two officers at the front station observing the room. Then he turned before they pointed and headed directly to the table Cain sat at.

There was no cordial greeting, just a stare from each man into the other's eyes. The prisoner had the bluest, most familiar eyes. Eyes that said things Cain preferred not to know.

"I smelled you before you ever entered the prison." The prisoner sat back folding his arms. "Very curious," his eyes narrowed. Then leaning forward he breathed in, seeming to savor Cain's scent. Like a wine taster he appeared to roll the flavor around in his mouth. He closed his eyes, his forehead wrinkled, then his eyes popped open as if something surprised him.

"You are old as I. Just about," he corrected. blinking his blue eyes rapidly. "But you can't be Kind. And, you are weak." He pondered, tapping a finger on the table before adding, "You've been sleeping."

Cain was sure this was one of the two men with dreadlocks that spoke to his father that night he was a boy, the night he'd wandered in on their conversation. The voice, the eyes, told all.

"Yes, I have been asleep," Cain replied.

Both vampires reviewed each other carefully. But the older was tentative, and curious about something else. The wrinkles in his face hardened like wire cords. His eyes seemed to sparkle between blue and green.

Placing both hands flat on the table the man breathed in Cain's scent again.

"Why do you wear the ropes?"

"Ropes?" Cain questioned with a sideways glance.

The other man gave a hardy chuckle, running his tongue along his upper teeth that seemed sharper than they should have been. "What do you call yourself?"

"Cain Wander."

"Cain," he muttered in a peculiar tone. He was turning something over in his mind. Cain felt a push toward his mind but the voices in his head helped him repell the entry.

"And why do you call yourself, Cain?"

"Because it is close to my true name."

The old man looked off dreamily. "Yes it is, isn't it?"

"Why do you subject yourself to this?" Cain could not resist asking.

The man looked at him, twisting his neck as he leaned closer. "What da real difference it make when ya eternal?" he shrugged. "Tomorrow who no what me do?"

Cain looked at him with admiration. He had almost forgotten how good the old tongue sounded. "Ah ya, me had forgotten how good it be to be wit me own kin."

"Kheyang, a ya not?"

"I am."

"Dhen we are true kin indeed. We are Kind."

Cain grew silent.

"What boyaa?"

"Me not no notin of dhat," Cain admitted.

The other's brow wrinkled in puzzlement. "Notin? Who turn ya droo?"

Cain shrugged. "Me no notin. Not even what a turn is? Not even ya name."

Switching from their native tongue, Richard said, "I am Thori. Our people are from one of the few planets where highly complex life-forms developed first in the entire universe. This world here, this is primitive.

"Where we came from it was common knowledge that there was life on other worlds. But the further away we went from the epicenter of our world, the less chance there was of life forming at all, and when it did it was eons behind."

As the minutes went on Cain learned more about his people than he ever had from his father and he hung to Thori's every word.

"The planet where our kind began, was called, Zim. We are known as Zimri, a once peaceful and highly advanced society. One that believed in science, and it was that science that made it happen.

"A virus was formed through experimentation with longevity and it ravaged our world, killing billions of us in a matter of weeks. The few of us that survived were all but guaranteed extinction because we were sterile.

"It was all just the beginning. Those who lived had been infected. But for some reason our bodies were able to work with the virus and instead of killing us, it gave us regeneration powers, and decreased aging."

Cain noticed a red tear form in Thori's eyes. He handed him a napkin. Thori thanked him with a nod and wiped the blood away.

He continued: "For awhile we buried our dead, rebuilt, and things were fine. Until the hunger came. The starvation."

"Yes, I understand the starvation," Cain pursed his lips.

"We turned on each other, Cain. We ate each other," Thori said with disgust. "The blood gave us, the victors, new power," he smacked. "But there were so few of us left. Maybe hundreds, if that. We couldn't continue devouring ourselves.

"Something had to be done and so we learned to infiltrate others worlds blending with their people, and feeding on them at will. Then we learned how to rule over them by flooding their societies with superstitions, religions…it's all the same. It served a purpose.

"It made us angels, gods, feared, revered- served. Because where there is strife, a savior rules. We created the strife, and the savior. We made the devil and god.

"We took morality, and gave it. Our secret society thrived on whatever planet we invaded. And ate, and ate. And we ate."

Thori ran his tongue around the inside of his mouth. "We were young and had no control, no wisdom to govern our new existence. And just about when we started to make rules for ourselves, just as order came about, we discovered we could turn others.

"Not being able to procreate, it was our only way to have children. There were mass turnings and we called them Kindred. It was out of control. With Kindred growing, deaths on planets accelerated beyond wonder. More worlds were invaded. These worlds died quickly. The Kindred were young and hungry. They had absolutely no control. We even lost control of them, the millions of them that were made.

"Then war erupted between Kind and Kindred. We, the aged, the powerful, against the young, vulnerable, but murderous. Worlds were devoured, and brethren went against brethren…it only grew worse.

"We, the Kind, are called so because we were the original Zimri. We made it forbidden to turn, and if so, only under our law. The law is divine. The law is our survival.

"Now, the wars between us only lasted a few hundred years. We destroyed many of the Kindred and the remaining ones submit to the law. But the damage was done.

"So many worlds were ravaged, destroyed in the interim. We had to form parties of life scouts to search for inhabited worlds, our food source. Your father, Domm, was one such life scout. I was part of his crew. There were one thousand of us, a few hundred Kind, and the rest Kindred.

"Your father saved us. He found the last remaining world where human life existed and we made a decision not to send word back to the others. If the others came the food source would not last.

"We let them starve to death."

"So we can die?" Cain remarked.

"Oh yes, we can," Thori assured.

"But I went thousands of years without eating." Cain added.

Thori chuckled. "That I don't understand. But I suspect you will find those answers. Which will be on your own."

"Why?" Cain inquired

Ignoring his question. "Your father…" he paused. "Your mother is of a very ancient and immortal race from another dimension. This is how you and your twin became about. This is why you are different but you are still, Kind," Thori assured. "And this world we live in is the *last red paradise.*"

"Where was I born?"

"On the ship, on the way here." Thori looked at Cain and switched topics. "Do you remember the struggle between you and your father?"

"No, nothing," Cain nodded. "Well, just that there was a struggle."

Thori stared at him. "Do you know the condition of your father now?"

"The condition? You mean he lives?"

"Mostly sleeps."

Cain pounded the table and stood in anger. People around them took notice, including the two officers.

"Calm yourself and sit," Thori demanded in an even, lowered tone.

Cain sat, and people went back to talking. The officers kept a closer eye on them.

"Yes, your father and mother live. She is buried beside him. His body is missing its head and heart." Thori grinned. He found it humorous. "But where they are kept, no one knows." He paused. "But you..." Thori looked at Cain waiting for a response.

"But I?"

"Oh, yes," Thori assured, very pleased about something.

The Prophecy

"Stace!" a guard barked, racking his cell door.

The old vampire was already standing. An hour earlier he was told to pack his property and so he expected them to come for him soon.

Thori picked up his box of belongings and one of the two guards who came for him grabbed him by the arm, pulling him from the tiny cell. "Let's go," he spat, giving him a menacing stare.

Thori smirked, kept his cool and was escorted to Receiving and Release where he was stripped and searched.

"Run your fingers through your hair," a guard said in a bored tone just before he spit chew into a coffee mug. "Turn around. Bend your ass over." Thori complied. "Cough."

Once done with the routine the guard threw Thori a bright red jumpsuit with "Prisoner" stamped on the back in bold black letters.

After Thori was dressed, another burly guard shackled his hands and feet before handing the prisoner to federal agents in dark suits. The agents escorted the chained and shuffling vampire to a black van with dark tinted windows. They loaded him into a cage in the back and locked it. The agents, then took the front seats and slid on dark shades. The driver chewed gum vigorously. The passenger put a Sting CD on.

As they pulled out, Thori noticed a black Ford SUV in front and another behind the van as they left the prison. He got comfortable, expecting the ride to be long. Transfers always came as a surprise and always were long trips.

Hours later, and on a back road between beautiful tall and green trees. Thori figured he'd pluck where they were headed out of the driver's head. He was bored and had nothing else to do but the information was blocked.

A wrinkle creased Thori's forehead. "Who are you men?" He leaned forward, chains rattling.

The agent on the passenger side turned and fired a tranquilizer dart hitting Thori in the neck. Which only seemed to really piss him off.

"We have a situation," the driver radioed to the lead vehicle!

Breaking free of his chains like they were threads, Thori's eyes turned black. His fangs grew long and dripped a clear liquid.

"He's not happy and the serum is taking its time to work," The passenger drew his side-arm.

With a roar Thori pulled on the front cage door, warping the frame.

"Shoot him!" the driver shouted, swerving to the left before regaining control.

The other agent fired. But Thori avoided each round. Again he fired, this time as Thori completely pulled the door of the cage inward. It was the distraction the agent needed, and bullets tore off the left half of Thori's face.

The vampire grabbed the agent by the throat with a single hand and yanked him into the cage. The man struggled to break free, all while Thori's face healed in an instant.

Grinning, Thori slammed his victim about the cage like a rag-doll.

"Carter, Carter!" the driver shouted, stepping on the gas and swerving left and right to get the vampire off his friend. He didn't hear the shouts of his superior over the radio shouting for him to stop the van.

Carter's blood curdling screams as Thori sank his teeth into his throat slow and calculated caused the driver to reach for his gun. But by then Thori had drained all of his life fluids.

Thori turned his attention to the driver who attempted to steer with one hand and shoot with the other. Then he leapt at him with a monstrous cry.

Again the van swerved, this time to the right with the tires screeching. The back window was shot out. The van flipped, rolled, and slid along its side. Sparks flew with the friction.

Both accompanying SUVs screeched to a holt. Four agents exited each vehicle, guns pointed.

"Did they get him with the tranquilizer?" one agent asked.

"We're screwed if they didn't."

"Shh," another waved as they tentatively inched closer to the van. "Drex, Carter," he called. Nothing.

Agents lined up along the roof of the van that lay on its side while others lined up along its underbelly. The senior agent signaled, and an agent peeked around through the rear window of the van.

"I didn't see a thing," he whispered.

"Well look again. They're in there," the agent next to him urged.

With a grunt, the agent looked again. In a blur of motion, a hand snatched him through the glass. He screamed. The van rocked. Agents reacted with gunfire. Thori blasted through the front windshield and rolled to the ground as the fire rocketed in his direction. His body was riddled with bullets and he danced to the ground falling flat on his back in spasms.

"Will he die?" one agent reloaded and stood over the jerking body.

"Not one as old as him. Matter of fact if it wasn't for the serum these bullets wouldn't have made a difference."

"Yea, but they're silver, and liquidate upon contact so it runs through his system."

"True, but it is the poison that makes all the difference." The agent pulled out a cell phone and called for back up and a clean up team.

"Drexler and Carter are gone." An agent had pulled their bodies from the wreckage.

"So is Brown," said another, pulling his body out as well.

The senior agent was still on the phone talking to a superior; his demeanor grew grave. "Damn it," he turned. "How did the agents die?" he shouted to the others.

"Looks like he fed off them," was the reply. The victims were pale and emaciated.

Immediately the senior agent ran for the front SUV which was thirty yards away. Once there he fumbled around through the back of the inside of the vehicle.

He couldn't find the medical kit. "Everybody, pull back. Now!" he cried.

"What's chief talking about?" the young agent who stood next to Thori asked. It was at that moment that Thori stirred. There was barely time for the man to pull out his weapon before Thori's hand snatched his ankle and pulled him down. It was a short struggle. In a flash Thori's teeth sunk in the agent's jugular.

In the meantime another of the men drew a buck-knife and reached for Thori's neck and cut a deep wound. As the blood squirted, Thori gargled and gasped for air. With a sawing motion the agent kept going until he removed Thori's head from his body.

"Son-of-a-bitch!" Another agent went to his knees and hurled his breakfast all over the pavement.

Thori's body collapsed in lifelessness, his black eyes fixed in death.

"Oh my God, no." The senior agent slowly drew his gun as he spoke.

"What do you mean, Chief? I killed him," the man holding the bloody knife held his head up and grinned. "Piece of cake."

"Looks like they can die," another smirked.

"Don't anybody move," the chief warned.

"Boss," an agent stepped forward and the chief downed him with a single round to the forehead. The silver liquid oozed out of the hole in his head.

Don Atchison

"My God, why'd you do that?" another agent went for the downed man.

"I said nobody fucking make a move!"

"Boss, put down the gun."

"Listen, you idiots. That vampire isn't dead. He's inside of one of us, right now."

Fearful stares went from agent to agent. There were six of them left. Everyone went still.

"Did you see that?" an agent freaked. "It was like a light."

Something translucent leapt into the agent who still held the severed head. He dropped it and attacked another agent who shot him in the stomach. But that translucent form went from him to the shooter who now turned upon his associates

Bullets flew back and forth as the agents turned on themselves until none were left. Then the translucent form went into the body of Thori and it stood, and went for the severed head. Picking up the bloodied part, the body attached the head and Thori screamed. He then fell to his knees and inhaled, gasped, and stood coughing. But alive and whole.

Just as he stood, five vampires smoothly landed from the sky, surrounding him.

"Kindred," Thori hissed. He was weak. He needed blood from the living.

"Very old Kindred, and we outnumber you," one grinned. They all wore black leather outfits. "You are too weak to defeat us. So you will -"

Before another word could escape his mouth Thori had moved and in an instant sunk his fangs into his neck. The vampire screamed, at first from surprise, then pain, and finally horror as he was totally drained.

As soon as there was no blood left Thori's victim turned to stone then exploded into millions of smaller rocks and dust.

The other four stepped back in fear. "You dare?" Thori sneered. His eyes went black. The Kindred had been right about one thing, he was old, and now his blood had him feeling stronger than ever.

"Bow down!" Thori demanded, and at once the kindred knelt on one knee, heads lowered in reverence.

Thori spat, "How little respect your kind have for your elders is an abomination." Closing his eyes, dropping his head back, he opened and clenched his fists. The thought of Cain was on his mind. Would he, could he find the First Father? And in time?

Breathing in and out deeply, Thori sensed apocalyptic times in the air. Cain's survival and appearance all but sealed that.

The prophecy was real. Things were about to change.

Thori took to the sky, and his four new minions, followed behind him.

Part II

The Witch

1968: It was a Pan American flight from New Orleans to Norfolk, Virginia. A beautiful, dark skinned woman in a casual knee-high dress and flared straw hat was one of the first to board. She took a window seat near the wing and removed her dark, over-sized shades and hat. Her head turned to the window. The tarmac bristled with luggage handlers and other workers as planes landed and took off.

Before long, a male passenger placed his carry on bag in the compartment above the vixen, and sat beside her. "Looks like we'll be neighbors for awhile," he flirted.

She smiled. "Seems so." Then she turned her attention back to the window.

"My name is Charles Benedict," he brushed a hand over her knee as he held it out to shake.

Musing over the flirtatious and bold move, she tilted her head. Then with a firm grip shook his hand saying, "Helena." She pulled out a stick of Wrigley's gum and plopped it in her mouth.

"Well, Helena," he was captivated by the soft curvature of her jaw as it rotated when she chewed, "that's a pretty name. Do you fly often?"

"This is my very first time on an airplane."

Charles leaned close. "Oh, really," he smiled. "Well deary, there is absolutely nothing to it." He pat her exposed knee, giving it a slight squeeze.

"I don't know," she said, pursing her lip." I'm sort of nervous."

He grinned. "I'll keep you safe," he boasted, taking her hand and kissing it. She noticed a Free Mason ring on one of his fingers.

"And how do you propose to do that?" she jested.

"I have my ways. I'm like a magician," he teased, raising a brow.

The pilot greeted everyone aboard the flight, and the flight attendants asked everyone to buckle up.

"Magic? Oh, I knew it," Helena slapped his shoulder. "Are you a New Orleans native?" she giggled sweetly.

"Born and raised in England, honey." Charles raised his chin. "And you? From your accent you sound French."

"I'm from Paris. But I have family here." She looked into his eyes. Many secrets seemed to dance in them, and her stare narrowed as she read them with ease.

Their plane taxied down the runway and took off and Charles gave her a comforting look. He held her hand for reassurance. "We'll feel a little bump or two but that's called turbulence. It's normal."

Helena had a worried look, and only nodded to acknowledge his remark.

"I love New Orleans," she said dreamily as she looked down at the tiny city below. "The city itself seems to live in a way that's hard to explain."

"I know just what you mean. New Orleans certainly does seem to live. Even the dead," Charles joked.

Flashing an amused look, she replied, "I think I agree with you Charles."

"I'm an agreeable man." He liked the way she said his name, imagining how it would sound coming from her as they made love. He looked at her red lips, and the lines of her neck. He wanted her.

"Well, you seem agreeable enough."

"Much more than you think. Helena, you and I could have a great time together."

"Really?"

"Yes. I could take you places no man ever has before," he licked his lips, thinking of how he'd also love to share her. To watch other men as they fucked her brains out and she cried in ecstasy.

She snickered. "You are so terrible."

"You have no idea," he bragged. "But you're a big girl aren't you? I'm a big boy."

Helena looked out the window. Everything below was so small.

Easing up a little, he decided to change topics. "So what has you headed for Virginia?"

"Business. And you?"

A stewardess walked the aisle.

"Business as well."

"Queer feeling, being up so high." Helena perspired a little. "Maybe I should go to the restroom to freshen up," she said as she unbuckled.

"I can go with you," he winked.

She giggled but nodded for him to accompany her. Once inside the tiny restroom he wiped her face with a cool, wet towel. Their eyes connected, and they kissed, slow. Then savagely.

Charles grappled her breasts; while she fumbled with his zipper. They kissed more. She pulled out his hard throbbing dick. He kissed her harder, and went to remove her dress but she slid to her knees, and rubbed her face over his pulsating shaft.

"Oh yes," he looked down at the woman, straddled her face, holding the back of her head, and slid his dick in her mouth.

She knew right what to do and immediately her hands grabbed each cheek of his ass and her head bobbed back and forth as she sucked like a vacuum.

It didn't take long for Charles to start gyrating in her mouth, forcing the tip of his knob till he felt the push of the back of her throat.

Once again she surprised him and didn't gag at all. She only shifted her jaw and was able to swallow him whole.

Flight 7107 left on time from New Orleans at 8:15 a.m., February 23, 1968. A few hours later the senior pilot reported minor icing on the windshield though the weather was otherwise clear. Shortly afterwards, he called in due to minor engine problems.

Somewhere over the Appalachian Mountains flight 7107, headed for Virginia, sent out a distress call. The next day the plane was found scattered over the mountain-side. All one hundred and thirty seven passengers and six crew were reported to have lost their lives.

Charles woke, blurry-eyed, in a room lit solely by moonlight that shone through an open window. The curtains flapped occasionally as a cool breeze generously flowed through. A wood chime tinkled on the porch. *"Somewhere over the rainbow,"* played on a scratchy record in another room in the house. Footsteps creaked over the wooden floor in the hallway outside the room.

Startled by his surroundings, Charles leapt out of bed. He had not a stitch of clothing on, and his heart pumped with fear. The last thing he recalled was his head between his knees and a stewardess shouting instructions. A buzzer had been ringing like crazy and the plane he was on shook with violence he had never experienced.

He blinked. Slowly, his eyes adjusted to the darkness and he realized a figure sat in the darkness by the only door in the room.

"Who are you?" he squinted, too wary to move any closer.

"You hurt my feelings," said a soft voice. The woman's tone was tinged with humor. She stood and stepped into the light.

Charles fell back onto the bed. "You," he choked.

"Little, ole me. Yes," she posed, hands on hips. She was wearing the dress he had seen her in before. The skirt hem fluttered as wind blew through the window.

"What's going on? How did I get here? Where am I?
The last thing I remember -"

"Was the plane going down." Imitating the downward
slide of the plane with her hand, she ended with a "Boom." Then
she laughed again, shifting one hip outward.

Swaying with arrogance, Helena said with contempt,
"You cried like a baby. You didn't keep me safe at all," she
pouted. "But I kept you safe." She stepped forward with a mad
look in her eyes. Her gaze was full of threats. Her voice sounded
more aged.

In one quick motion she lifted her dress over her head and
tossed it to the ground. Charles was bewitched. Her body was
perfect. Her breasts, C-size. Areolas dark. Her hips were just
wide enough, and plump enough to squeeze. While her medium
length hair was long enough to yank in the heat of passion, it was
much greyer than before. That long soft neck of hers was inviting. Her red lips glistened under the moon's beams. They were
slightly parted, and seemed to whisper, "Charles."

Helena approached.

"What are you doing?" He instinctively stepped backwards.

"You're a big boy. Don't you know?" She had a lascivious stare. Her voice was now that of an old woman.

"How did we survive?"

Licking her lips, she mounted Charles, who even though
terrified, had a stiff dick. "What makes you so sure we did?" She
kissed his forehead, shifted, and maneuvered his dick inside her
in one smooth motion.

Sitting straight up, with Charles laying flat, she grinded
her hips like only an experienced woman could.

"Damn it," he grunted, and reached up to fondle her
bouncing breasts. They were firm and soft at the same time. He
ran his fingers over her erect nipples and flicked them between
thumb and forefinger.

She swayed her head and moaned. "I want you to listen to me carefully," she said as she kept moving over him.

"Yes, yes."

"What is most important right now is that you are about to receive a fuck like never before." She fell forward and licked the side of his face, then sat up and rode him like a bull-rider, swinging one arm in the air. Her face glowed white.

"Ride it," he groaned out between clenched teeth, thrusting upward in sync with her. "Take it all," he groaned. Her juices saturated his groin.

She spun and leaned forward, giving him a view of his dick in her pussy. She slowed her pace, swallowing him and releasing him in rhythmic strokes. In and out. In and out.

"You like the way that looks?" she looked back, tongue dangling.

"Yes," he said breathlessly. He slapped her ass.

"Is this what you want?" She clenched his ankles and bounced harder.

"Oh, yes. I do," his head fell back. "Ooh! Damn," he gasped. "You are so tight, so deep."

She spun again. His penis never slid out. She drew back and slapped him hard across the face then rode him so hard and fast the bed rocked and squeaked.

Somewhere over the rainbow, still played, louder this time.

She slapped him again. Charles didn't know it, but there was a dark glow that covered his face. Helena grinned, she was working a spell over him.

Charles was on the verge of ejaculating. He pulled her down, locking his arms around her and thrusting upward with no reserve.

"Good boy. Good boy," she panted.

He roared and flipped her over. Her legs rode his shoulders and he pounded her like a madman.

"Yes, fuck me good," she screamed.

Somewhere over the rainbow.

He lift and slammed her head into the pillows. His ass gyrated quicker. She bit him on the chest and licked the blood. Her teeth grew sharper and longer.

He pumped harder, faster. The bed rocked. Footsteps sounded in the hall.

Somewhere over the rainbow.

Charles pinned her ankles on each side of her head and she screamed with pleasure. Then Charles screamed. He shrieked, he shivered. A load of thick cum filled her body. Helena laughed. Charles laughed.

When they were done, she pushed him away and went to the window. She looked out at the full moon and leaned, leaning on the window seal, her face washed in satisfaction. Charles admired her smooth, glistening body and locked on the moisture that still seeped down her legs. His handy work.

Finally, she whirled around and spoke. "Your miserable little life was spared so that you could serve me and my purposes."

"What? Uh…" Charles sat up, flummoxed.

In an instant she was upon him and threw him across the room. He slammed into the wall and stumbled to his feet.

Again she was upon him, her eyes boring into his. Deep inside them Charles saw something that made him grimace. He realized she sounded old. Her hair was fully grey. He fell to the ground, cowering. All he could think about was what he saw in those terrible orbs. She wasn't human. Wasn't even sure she was a female.

Helena headed for the door. "Your clothes are on the side of the bed. Get dressed. You have a flight to catch." With those words, she left the room.

Helena walked down the hallway deep in thought. Her focus was on the man she'd just left. She would give him the secrets to finding Cain, who would lead her to the First Father.

Doors needed to be opened. She would make it happen.

Epilogue

Vampires are a race of people like any other. They live they die. They are among us. They have been with us since our very beginning. Manipulating, controlling our cultures in order to survive. While we, none the wiser, in a quest to partake in immortality, have fallen prey to the very fables they've concocted. We believe, hoping that after death we will turn and ascend into being …

Immortal…and in paradise.

Heaven is here on Earth, just as Bob Marley told us.

The ancient king Mithridates of Portugal is said to have made himself totally immune to all poisons by treating himself to gradual doses. According to a story retold by poet A.E. Harsman:

They put arsenic in his meat
And stared aghast to watch him eat
They poured strychnine in his cup
And shook to see him drink up
I tell the tale I heard told
Mithridates, he died old

Mithridates, that ancient king, was a vampire, and he never died at all. The First Father. He is Adam. His queen is Eve. And they have secrets, one of which is that there are those who feed on vampires and such beings are a serious danger. They possess unimaginable power and magic. They are also immortal. They are witches. And they seek to live amongst us.

Excerpt from Second Son

Sitting up in a panic, she began to hyperventilate. A sense of calm swept over her only when she realized she was in a huge bed with thick, fluffy blankets and silk sheet.

The room was totally dark which meant nothing to a blind girl who had spent her entire life in darkness of many kinds.

"Who is there?" She gasped. "I can... I can hear you," she trailed off. All of her working senses were alert, searching for danger.

"It is I." Cain sat in a wooden rocker with hands crossed over his lap, watching. He could see perfectly in the dark.

The girl fingered her face. There was no swelling, no damage, no pain. She ran her tongue along her teeth, they were all there; as aligned as ever. At first she considered that maybe the assault had been a terrible dream. Her better sense knew it wasn't.

"What have you done to me?" she demanded.

"I saved you."

"Maybe I didn't want saving!" she snapped with force enough to surprise herself.

Cain gave no reply.

Tilting her head, she gasped," I can hear your heart beat." She placed her hand on her chest. "I can feel it. And... I can smell you." Her distress building, she begged to know, "What is wrong with me?"

Still no response from Cain.

"I'm afraid," she broke down.

Without a sound and in an instant Cain was beside the bed. A slight breeze blew across the girl's face from his advance.

"So fast, how?" she pushed away.

"You needn't be afraid. You need not fear anything anymore. You are safe with me."

The girl's heart racing, Cain smiled at her and her pulse slowed, falling in sync with his.

Summoning the courage, she requested. "Sit next to me."

Cain obliged, and the youngster scooted nearer. Obviously tentative. She ran fingers over Cain's warm face. It was her way of seeing.

She felt stubble, and his skin was smooth, but something was off. "What are you?"

"Am angel," he joked.

She felt his lips vibrate and curl upward. She withdrew her hands, smiling. "And what am I?" she asked.

"A most beautiful angel. A goddess."

That ignited a melodic giggle. "Will I be able to fly?" She asked with sarcasm.

Cain's soul warmed and he laughed with his whole inner being. "As high as the mountains rise or as deep into the valleys your strength can carry you. You will learn to fly."

"Great," she pulled Cain to lay with her. He sensed she trusted him as they embraced. He knew he would protect her and peered into her mind seeing much of her troubled past.

Cain decided that for her there would be no more foster homes. No more sexual abuse in the name of love. No more beatings and having to run away. She'd no longer have to pray to an unanswering god, one that never intervened to stop the pain.

No more false promises or outright lies.

The youth was now in the arms of safety and privileged existence. She was home.

Kaila Jones was no more. Now she was Kaila Wander, a vampire, a Kindred, daughter of Kheyang.

About the Author

Donald W. Atchison, Jr. was born and raised in San Diego, California. He currently resides in Atlanta, Georgia with his wife and son.